RAFINA

RAFINA

A Novella

Shandana Minhas

PICADOR INDIA

First published 2018 by Picador India
an imprint of Pan Macmillan Publishing India Private Limited
707, Kailash Building
26, K.G. Marg, New Delhi – 110 001
www.panmacmillan.co.in

Pan Macmillan, 20 New Wharf Road, London N1 9RR
Basingstoke and Oxford
Associated companies throughout the world
www.panmacmillan.com

ISBN 978-93-86215-38-3

This is a work of fiction. All characters, locations and events are fictitious. Any resemblance to actual events or locales or persons, living or dead, is entirely coincidental.

1 3 5 7 9 8 6 4 2

Typeset by R. Ajith Kumar, New Delhi
Printed and bound in India by
Replika Press Pvt. Ltd.

1

'IT'S THE NAME, Naz, it's the name. Who told you to call her Rafina? Sounds like a dancer in the movies. After Helen … Rafina! No wonder she's such a dramaybaaz.'

Rafina scowled in the direction of her mother and aunt, engrossed in their bashing session in the front room, and slammed a plate into the drying rack. But the plate was tin, the rack plastic and empty, and the pigeon perched on the concrete lattice above the sink wasn't moved enough to object on her behalf either. Rafina hmphed. *When I'm somebody, that nobody will change her tune.*

When she was younger and still bothered asking why life was so clearly tilted in favour of men, her father had told her it was because men read the papers, and women wasted their time reading each other, even though they were blank pages. She wasn't going to make that mistake. She'd keep all the gossips out of her life.

She flicked a finger at the pigeon preening above her – *fat ass must be Rosie khala's sister* – and it flew off with an indignant gurgle. Her view of card girl was still broken though, so after she finished the rest of the dishes that had been piled and left to rob her morning, she squeezed through the half-door between the kitchen area and the bathroom to go directly into the family's bedroom. Two minutes later she was at her window looking at the burnished face on the billboard looming above her, mockery already forgotten as she locked eyes with the glamorous woman selling phone cards.

It was a two-room police quarter on the third floor of a services compound, but from the vantage of that window it felt like the top of the world. Though she shared the room with her mother and brother, Rafina spent a good chunk of her day staring out of the window and felt a certain ownership. Nothing rested on its sill but her elbows. Right at the corner of Gomery police quarters, it gave her an unobstructed view of the intersection between Gomery Street, M. A. Jinnah Road, and the new pedestrian bridge across the wide road over which card girl had been suspended.

The bridge was a new addition to the cityscape. It had been inaugurated last year by a man in a suit, who had stood firmly in the centre of the main road – like the people whose deaths had prompted the need for some other way to cross – with a brass band playing around him, and kept his back to the spiderweb of streets and alleys on either side the entire time. If she had a spare egg, which she didn't, and a grenade launcher, Rafina would have shot out at him with a flick of her delicate, malnourished wrist. He could have at least given the people of the byways some acknowledgement. She could have given him a tour, if he had looked up and asked. She knew the road. She liked the road. She liked its proximity.

The headlights from the cars that fed the road, illuminated her bedroom walls at night and made it easier to pretend the room was a stage. She would dance away from the sound of her mother snoring and the poisonous exhalations of her younger brother's rectum. The flow of the traffic was her familiar, her applause. The throbbing of heavy engines excited her. Their growl was her growl.

After the bridge was inaugurated she fantasized that a man in a big car, slowing to admire the smooth, unblemished lines of the new erection, would spot her at the window, be enraptured by her beauty and feel compelled to make that journey a thousand times a day in the hopes of seeing her again. But her fantasies tended to end there. She had grown up to the stifled sounds of her parents writhing together under a quilt, but there wasn't space enough to stretch her own limbs. And she hadn't felt any desire to either since the wrench in the stomach she had felt when the silky-moustached Deputy Superintendent she used to watch from the window had walked authoritatively into their quarter last year, barely pausing to knock. Life had been unfair then too; she had felt her mouth go dry as she realized he had come to tell them her father was dead.

Earlier, she had wanted to feel more. She used to feel a quickening in her pulse when he was in sight; a thrill would rise in her as he stepped out of his four-wheel drive in his freshly ironed uniform, walked into the police station with clots of humanity around him radiating something she didn't have a word for.

But when he finally came to her – and how she had hoped he would – it was to bring sorrow.

She hadn't felt anything when he'd called out to her weeks later as she was walking down the street. The police mobile had slowed as he'd leaned out and asked how she was doing. The encounter wasn't long after his lackey had told her mother they had to vacate their home by the end of the year and she'd responded flatly: 'Meray dil main luddoo phoot rahay hain; I'm so happy, I can barely contain myself.'

Maybe it had been her eyes, she thought later. Why else would he stammer and look away? Send the same lackey at night to tell them he'd fixed it so they could stay another year?

She'd tested her theory on the boys around the compound, and a couple of times on men in the street till one of them followed her from the corner shop until he saw her walk through the gate under the MONTGOMERY STREET POLICE STATION sign. Watching his smug face cloud with fear was almost worth the eyes that had tried to undress her as she made her way to the back of the police station and through the gap in the wall that connected it to the staff quarters on the lane behind, which had their own unobtrusive entrance with a handwritten 'Gomery quarters' tacked on one side.

Further experiments after school confirmed it. She now knew her eyes were the prettiest eyes for miles till the bridge and the billboard rose and brought her competition, and renewed desire.

Rafina wanted again. But what she wanted was to rise above it all, and loom over the world like the woman in the phone card advertisement. That, she felt, would be just about the best thing that could ever happen to her. Everyone would know her. Everyone would admire her. No one would tell her what to do. Even Rosie khala's raspy voice – there it was sawing through the door of her room again – would be drowned by the adulation she would one day inspire.

'How did she take the news?' The pigeon was grilling her mother. 'She must have cried.'

'No, she didn't. She's not fussy all the time; sometimes she listens to her Ma.'

Of course I do, Rafina thought. *Where's the room in this hole for disagreement? Like I could have said no.*

But she didn't really mean it. Not being able to go to college didn't bother her as much as it might once have. Ma had a B.Sc in Home Economics, didn't she? It hadn't quite taken her to the manager's cubicle on the factory floor. Rafina knew she was destined for bigger things.

'What are you going to do with her now?' Rosie khala just wouldn't let it be. If she'd had a son, Rafina might have thought this was leading up to a proposal of some sort, but Rosie's son had died at twelve. They'd gone to the village and he'd choked to death before they could get him to a hospital. Bad air, Zeenat had told Rafina when she'd asked what had happened to him. He'd died of village air. *Oh! She meant asthma! How did a stupid like her get into college?*

Was Khala perhaps interrogating in hopes of a match for a cousin? A brother? Rosie khala never mentioned her extended family, just yakked about her dear departed mother, who Rafina imagined must have dropped dead the first time Rosie beti had dyed her hair the colour of gajar ka halwa. Who would believe someone so out of touch was in the business of beauty?

Rosie worked in a ladies' parlour; she always emphasized 'ladies' when she met someone for the first time. Rafina had found it funny at first. Then she'd overheard her telling Ma about several businesses in Defence that were really massage dens full of plump, yielding Punjabi women who had floated down river on their buoyant bosoms. Defence was the most expensive part of town, and Rosie had been nudging Naz to nudge hubby to get a transfer because that way collection would be more lucrative.

'Punjabis,' Rafina's mother said, deflecting the attempt, 'they get all the jobs.' Mother and aunty tittered like schoolgirls, but Rafina hadn't got the joke. *Must be an old woman thing.* They got softer in the head as they grew older, not just in the stomach. Last month Rafina had caught Ma standing in front of the large portrait of her father that hung over the entrance door and laughing till the tears ran down her face. It was very early in the morning; even the dogs weren't running for their refuges yet – she must have thought her children were asleep. Rafina watched her from the doorway of the inner room and vowed she wasn't going to be like that when she grew older. She wasn't going to be fat either.

'I thought she could start coming to work with me. One of the women is on maternity leave for a month and the shift supervisor said she could fill in for her. If she gets a little experience now, maybe she will be able to get a full-time slot at the factory when one opens up.' Rafina's mother worked at a garment factory, preparing denims for export. She said it was a good job, better than most a woman like her could ever get. But Rafina didn't buy it. She'd tried to talk her out of taking the job, told her they could live off her father's pension; hadn't the DSP mentioned that the dependents of a policeman killed in the line of duty got a payment and a pension? Ma had mutely shown her a piece of paper. Immediate relief paid to heirs of late personnel, it told them, was Rs 15,000. Monthly maintenance to widows and dependent children of late personnel, it continued, was Rs 3000. Rafina lingered on the last line: 'Marriage grant (on marriage of first and second daughters only) Rs 10,000 (non-refundable).'

'I can get married,' she had blurted. Naz had looked down at the paper again, up at her teenage daughter in silence, and down once more, then fixed her stare on Rafina for what felt like hours, taking in the length of her—her unbowed shoulders, the frighteningly precise features, the spark in her eyes, her dark skin, and asked:

'How many times?'

After another long silence in which they considered each other, saw each other, and chose to reach for each other, they had laughed till her brother had woken up and complained about their yowling. Neither had brought up the factory's disadvantages, or Rafina's marital potential, ever since.

Her mother's skin had turned grey shortly after she started work. The fumes from the machines, the wisps of fabric, the lack of ventilation: they couldn't quite tell what it was. Ma said it happened to everyone. Rafina had tried buying her a whitening face wash – a genuine one recommended by Rosie – (not fakes like the ones sold by the Pathan down the road), and badgering her every day into using it after she came home from work. It made no difference. Neither did the oatmeal scrub or the yoghurt and lime mask Rosie insisted on making for her friend.

The skin remained grey, casting her in shadow even in the sunlight.

After watching a particularly moving episode of a TV drama on the neighbour's television the night before, Rafina had told Ma to stay home, that she'd go to the factory instead. Her relief when her mother stroked her hair and asked her if she'd been watching TV again was instant and secret. She had realized right after the words were spoken that she wasn't about to work in that factory, not if that was what would happen to her own smooth skin. She would rather clean other people's toilets if it came to that. Not that she'd have to, once her plan for the future fell into place.

But Rosie khala had shown up that morning and, to her horror, in the midst of discussing her dramaybaazi, they also talked about her actually going to work at the factory. And for once Rosie was talking sense.

'How you can even think it! You keep telling me you're being suffocated slowly. You want to take a delicate thing like her there – what kind of a mother are you?' Maybe, Rafina thought, she would forgive Rosie khala for that earlier remark about her name. She had probably been joking anyway; could a Rosina make fun of a Rafina?

'What choice do I have?' Ma snapped. 'I can't send

her to work somewhere else all by herself, now can I? You and I both know the stories her father told me.'

'He was just keeping you in line. I go here and there every day. So do you. It's not like someone is going to rush up and drag her into the fields.'

'We're women. She's a girl, and a decent looking one at that. Ripe fields or empty plots, people are the same, as Shaukat would say.'

'He never put six words together in front of me but ever since he passed it seems Shaukat never shut up.'

'Like you let a body speak. He had a lot to say. Policemen see a lot.'

'Or nobody ever listened to him at work.'

Rafina could hear the teasing.

'You know what he'd say about you?' Ma's tone was bland.

'What?'

'First-class ass. Third-class mouth.'

Not the girlish tittering again … Rafina snorted contemptuously. *Crude, crude, crude.*

'No more laughing now, my stomach hurts,' Rosie khala wheezed and began to cough. 'Give me some water; after that I have to get going.'

'But you just got here.'

'House appointment.'

Rosie khala supplemented what she earned from

her day job by providing the same services by taking house calls from clients she met at work. It was a dangerous thing because if the boss found out, she would fire Rosie immediately. But there was no way she could raise her girls—Zeenat, Kainat and Niamat—on the 7,000 rupees she earned working 11 to 7, six days a week with no transport allowance or anything. Her girls were like her, with healthy appetites and boisterous. Her husband was a driver for a charity ambulance service. Rafina had always thought him surprisingly cheerful for someone in a dead-end job. The whole family seemed to find life very amusing. Though Zeenat was too smug for her own good. If her own father hadn't been killed during an encounter, Rafina told herself, she would have gone on to college too. Not that she wanted to, she promptly reminded herself. She and Rosie khala's daughters were different. She was China Silk to their steel wool.

'So late? It's almost eight.' Rafina's attention returned to the conversation.

'Wedding season. Little blouses. The baji wants her tummy waxed and she's too busy to do it at the parlour. This one doesn't have a job so I think she's just shy. Don't know why; we see enough bearded women as it is, but who am I to spurn what the Creator offers?'

That set them off again. Rafina stopped picking at her dry cuticles long enough to roll her eyes. She leaned away from the window sill so she could look into the mirror on the wall by the bathroom and rolled them again, but it was impossible to follow the arc all the way through.

'At least let me give you something to eat before you go,' Ma said.

'No, no, I don't have time for anything, except maybe a cup of tea and one little paratha.'

Rafina heard the chair creak as Naz got up. She quietly closed the bathroom door so her mother wouldn't see her across the connecting room. Utensils rattled. A match was struck. Later Rafina would wonder if things would have been different had she not heard what Ma said next:

'If only she was like your Zeenat … there's no option for my Rafina but the factory.'

'Rosie khala!' Rafina flew through the door and thrust herself into the portly woman's surprised arms, successfully stifling the urge to wrinkle her nose at the odour of stale sweat that wafted from her wash-and-wear shalwar kameez.

'How are you, beti? Always so pretty, just like your name.'

Prettier than your beloved rat faces will ever be, you

hypocrite. Rafina thanked Rosie for the compliment, and admired the polka-dot print of her outfit and its slimming effect.

'What pretty lies you tell, Rafina! Teach my girls too, will you? Wretched creatures just come right out and say things. This morning I asked Kainat and Niamat which one of them wanted to come to work with me and they both said no. Just like that. No. Imagine! Did I work like a bitch all these years to have my puppies turn their noses up at me? Never, Niamat said, forever and never. What's so wrong with parlour jobs, someone tell me!'

'Rosie khala, why don't you get *me* a job at your parlour?'

Even Rafina was surprised at the words that tumbled out of her mouth. Yes, she had meant to say them, but not quite so soon. A little charming, a little wheedling, and once Rosie khala had been softened by little Rafina's simple-mindedness, then … not now, not like this. Had she wrecked her chances?

She couldn't tell. Rosie khala was looking at Rafina, her face blank. Ma had chosen to play bystander.

'You're too young,' Rosie khala said finally.

'I could pass for older,' Rafina said. And she could. Her symmetrical features could be fourteen or twenty-four. There was little about her that suggested she was actually seventeen.

'Are you suggesting I lie?'

Rafina said nothing. She turned to her mother in mute appeal, fixing her with an accusing look that spoke of constant, interminable, fathomless suffering for which she, her own mother, had been responsible. Every casual slap, every choice bit of meat given to her brother, every toy he wore out first, every first of every month on which his school fees and not hers had been paid—it was all there in her gaze.

'Do it,' her mother blurted, suddenly tearing her eyes from Rafina's. 'What will it matter if you tell a lie? You've done it before over smaller things.'

'Even if I lie about her age, the girl knows nothing about the business.'

'I can learn quickly. And I already know more than you think I do.'

'Really? Like what?'

'Threading. Waxing. Zeenat taught me.'

Zeenat and Rafina had been friends, once. Then they had grown apart because Zeenat liked to study and Rafina liked television and they were too old to plait each other's hair anymore and didn't they know that only happened on screen now? That's what they had told their mothers and everybody else who asked. *The boy had never liked Zeenat anyway.*

'I can make wax with lemon and sugar.'

Rosie khala snorted. 'We don't use that kind at the parlour. We only use imported fruit wax now. You can't make that, can you?'

'I can learn.'

'It comes in a tin from Dubai. Can you make the tin and the plane too?'

Rafina kept quiet. When she was rich and famous, she wouldn't try and make people feel small.

'I use the other kind in my home rounds though,' Rosie khala granted grudgingly. 'If you can do that as well as Zeenat does, maybe I can find a use for you yet. That girl has her first term coming up.'

Just like that, the door had been opened. Rafina tried not to let her delight show on her face. Soon she would be on that billboard, and Rosie khala wouldn't find it quite as easy to put her in her place anymore.

2

THE UGLINESS OF making things beautiful became apparent to Rafina early in her apprenticeship.

When she started making rounds with Rosie khala she found the work was hard, repetitive and brought her in touch with all manner of grossness: blackheads and whiteheads, ingrown hair baking in infected flesh, unbrushed teeth under mouths contorted for threading, bloodstains on panties as legs spread for waxing. But what really offended Rafina was the sheer waste of all the accoutrements money could buy on women so unfit for them.

Most of the women Rosie catered to were so ordinary Rafina felt disappointed for them; they lived in palatial homes and spacious apartments, had cars and drivers and maasis and maalis; they had expensive creams, unguents, masks; and yet they were no different from the women of the byways. Their preoccupations were the same. Their skin was the same. Skin that pitted, oozed, flaked off, curdled, festered, and changed shade from zone to zone. Sometimes the callouses on their feet rasped against clothing as they took their shoes off. Their hair was just as difficult to subdue.

Within the first week Rafina felt her ambition plant firmer roots. *These products, this house, that velvet waistcoat on that buffalo stance … If I have it,* when *I have it, I'll be worth it. Look at the size of her pores! And that behind … like there are dwarfs blowing balloons in her pockets.* Maybe Rosie was used to the injustice of it, but she made no comment and remained unforthcoming when Rafina tried to bring the matter up. Eventually Rafina kept quiet about it too. Rosie and her daughters, Rafina decided, were content where they were. They had low self-esteem, probably because they weren't anything to look at. There was nothing about them that was special, that stood out, that made people look at them in a crowd. But she knew she had the magic the women who spent so much on a few hours of intense maintenance sought. They were only trying to achieve what she had naturally. It was why the DSP had given them an extra year. It was why her brother's friend sent her that tacky card. The magic didn't yield when money called for it, it didn't care where someone lived, and it didn't care that her skin was two shades darker than the bleached bajis who polished their faces more often than they polished their dining tables. *That shoot I saw yesterday with that actress surrounded by those men. Everyone thinks she's so beautiful but she's so pale it's disgusting. Like one of those lizards in the water tank. I bet those men were paid to sit at her feet. When it's me in the picture they'll be there because they want to be there. And I'll hold a baby that's my own colour. At least it'll look like one of mine.*

'Rafina!' Her khala's tone jerked Rafina from her daydream and back into her present. The woman lying on a white sheet on a king-sized bed beneath them was scowling up at her and pointing accusingly at a patch of redness welling on her side.

'The wax is too hot, Rosie!'

'I'm so sorry, madam, it's this girl, she's a little nervous today because I told her what an important client you are to me and I guess she wanted to impress you with her speed.' Rosie khala's improvisation skills improved as Rafina's apprenticeship wore on.

'That's all well and good, but if it happens again you know I'm going to cut money.' The woman rolled back onto her stomach, and Rosie khala gave Rafina a killer look before settling back to finishing her side of the work, slapping the sticky wax onto the proffered flesh with a butter knife and then removing it with a piece of denim. Rafina knew she would hear more about this later. Rosie khala had been going out of her way looking for things to scold her about since she had started. A difficult task, Rafina felt, as she had a natural talent for the work and looked very graceful doing it too, extending her arm fully with the removal of each strip, feeling the way her bicep undulated and admiring the elegance of each motion.

'That would be fair,' Rosie khala muttered to the woman's dimpled bottom.

'It's important to be fair.' The words floated up from the pillow where the woman rested her face, which was turned to the side to protect the shiny gloss on her thin lips. *Why is she all dressed up for waxing? Her husband is at work.* Rosie khala briefed Rafina about each client before taking her on an appointment. *Who is she wearing shiny gloss for? Does she have an affair on with someone? If I finish quickly maybe I can ask that girl in the kitchen. She seems quite a talker.*

'Done,' Rafina yelped triumphantly as she whipped off the last bit of wax from near the woman's ankle, celebrating her rapid journey from the meticulous fumbling of the novice to the speed and grace of the old hand. *I bet it gives Zeenat sleepless nights when Rosie talks about me.* She began to roll up her denim strips and wipe the leftover wax from the butter knife when Rosie khala stopped her with a slight nod of the head.

The client sat up: 'Let me check.'

A light frown marring her pretty – *but so boring, not like mine; mine tells a story, hers is a lullaby* – face, the madam went over her legs with a fine toothcomb looking for hair. At one point she stuck her face so close to the skin in her effort to find a survivor that she looked as if she were licking herself. Rafina stifled a giggle. She had burst out laughing once at one of her earlier appointments when the client, a fat woman wearing velvet in the middle of summer – *how badly she smelled* – had farted when they parted her legs to get at the elusive hair on the upper inner thighs. The client had been very upset and asked them to leave immediately. Rosie khala had had to beg for forgiveness on her knees, dragging a reluctant Rafina down with her. Only the thought of the door slamming shut on her face so soon after opening had kept Rafina there. She'd had to do a little bit of begging herself, afterwards.

'I would never jeopardize your work, Rosie khala,' she had whimpered. 'I know how important it is and how you need it to keep your family going and educate your girls.'

'I don't think you do, Rafina,' Rosie khala had

again given her the look that the teen now suspected meant her khala was more tuned to her than she'd like. 'I don't know what you really think, but I'll give you the benefit of the doubt just this once. Once. I love your mother like a sister, but my family comes first. I won't lose a wealthy client because my chhota can't keep her mouth shut.'

Rafina had fumed inside at being called a chhota. She wasn't the runner at some dhaba. When, after a couple of months, she became somewhat indispensable to Rosie khala, she had suggested she be called an assistant instead.

'It sounds more professional – the clients will like that.'

Rosie khala had told her it sounded like someone was thinking too much of themselves, and the clients would laugh, but the next time they were waxing a young woman's 'underlegs' in preparation for her cousin's mehndi, she said, 'Please meet my assistant.' The young woman had raised an eyebrow, nodded to the fluffy white cat asleep on the back rest of her sofa and said, 'Meet my boss.' Rafina would have scowled but she knew by then the underlegs required the most visible concentration and reverence to help the client relax. *It doesn't matter what she calls me; I'll only be doing this for a little while.* She wondered why the woman's crotch needed to be waxed in preparation for someone else's wedding, but kept the question to herself. She observed. She absorbed. One day she'd be moving in the same circles, and she wanted to be prepared.

That wasn't the first bikini wax Rafina had assisted with (merely handing Rosie khala things, of course, and never doing it herself – she wasn't experienced enough for that yet); there had been two other such occasions.

One of her first trips with her aunt had been to a spacious, double-storied house abutting Gizri in Clifton. A luscious address, like ice chips in the heat, it caressed her throat when she said the words. Rosie khala had mentioned there were two clients in the same family, a girl and her aunt.

'Just like us, Rosie khala.'

'Not quite, doll, not quite.'

'Why – are both of them hideous?'

Rosie laughed till she choked, and Rafina had to thump her on the back for a full minute.

The girl waiting for them in the foyer of the sprawling mansion – the guard at the gatehouse had made them wait while announcing them on the intercom, running his eyes up and down Rafina till Rosie asked him what he was looking at – had just graduated from college in America. She spoke a strange, jumbled language, English primarily, with bits from other tongues strewn here and there like landmines. Every once in a while the girl would insert an Urdu word that didn't belong and the whole sentence would explode. Rafina suspected her aunt understood even less of what the girl was saying than she did, but after a while she also started nodding every fifty seconds like Rosie. It seemed to be all that was required. The girl on the pink satin sheets continued to rattle off some story about graduation. There was a dog in it. Rafina wasn't sure if the dog was outside, if it had gone to college with her or was just someone she had met along the way.

'Next you have to do Aunty's waxing, haan?'

The 'haan' was like a pakora in a dish of ice cream. The school Rafina had gone to was English-medium, and when at home, she listened to all the English stations on her brother Kunwar's radio, but whatever language she had learnt or the RJs used, it was different from what some of these women spoke. Rafina studied the girl slyly as she pulled her low-cut jeans and a t-shirt back on. Jeans recently had been acting like shalwars: high-waist, low-waist, wide-pancha, narrow-pancha, and embroidered even. It was confusing. Rafina knew she needed to have regular access to some foreign magazines to stay current. Maybe once she started work at the parlour? *How to approach Rosie khala about that?* She picked up a couple of the glossies on the table by the girl's bedroom door before they were ushered elsewhere to wait –Rosie's frown was deepening. After half an hour of fidgeting on cane chairs in a veranda – she had flipped through all the pictures; she didn't want to let Rosie find out how slow a reader she was by spending twenty minutes on each page – Rafina asked aloud what was taking the aunty so long.

'Now, whatever happens, you keep your mouth shut, you hear?' came Rosie khala's cryptic reply.

A khansama arrived to escort them to a room in another wing and left them just inside it. A nurse pushed a wheelchair into the room, and Rafina got her first look at the aunty. An elderly woman with completely white hair, she appeared to be asleep in the chair. Her chin rested on her chest and a thin line of spittle leaked from a corner of her mouth. Her sleeveless shift revealed straw-like arms.

'Full body?' Rosie khala asked the nurse.

'And threading.'

'OK.' Rosie khala nodded to Rafina, and with the help of the nurse they moved the woman from her chair and laid her flat on her back on the bed.

Looking down at her, Rafina realized she was awake and paralyzed. One of Rafina's neighbours had a paralyzed mother. She was kept in a corner behind a curtain. Sometimes Rafina heard her moaning through the open door as she passed by.

Waxing a paralyzed woman was easier than she had expected but harder than it looked. There were none of the yelps of pain or requests for a break that some of the more spoiled clients were so fond of, but Rafina had to hold up the arms and legs so Rosie khala could wax them. And they couldn't turn her over because she would suffocate on the pillow. Rafina wanted to ask Rosie khala what they were doing and why. Why would a paralyzed woman need to be waxed? What important social event did she have to be part of? Was she a married paralyzed woman whose husband still loved her? Was there a good reason for this humiliation? Rafina could hardly contain herself.

'Is she married?' she blurted finally in the direction of the nurse, who was busy biting her nails in a corner.

'No,' the nurse replied.

'Did this just happen?'

'She's been like this for years.'

'Then why are we waxing her?'

'Because she likes to feel like a woman.'

'Did she say so?'

'She can't say anything; hasn't said a word since her accident.'

'Then how do you know she wants to be waxed?'

'Her sister says she does. She was very conscious of these things when she was younger.' The nurse got up and made a show of tucking in the bedspread again to indicate she was done talking about it. 'A woman has to look like a woman and feel like a woman,' she said.

The threading was a nightmare. Rafina did her best to stretch the skin for her aunt, but it was elastic and papery at the same time, and when Rosie was done, tiny red slashes were visible across the face. Rosie khala didn't seem perturbed; she had obviously done this before. And when dog girl came in to check, she looked at her aunt restored in her chair and cooed in delight.

'Don't you look beautiful!' she gushed to the top of her aunt's head, the chin having sunk back onto the chest. 'Why don't we go out and sit by the pool for a while so the dog can look at you and go woof woof?'

She paused in the doorway to give Rosie khala fifteen hundred rupees. They charged a standard five hundred for a full wax, except bikini of course – that was extra – so Rafina calculated that they were paid double for the paraplegic. The money would definitely be useful, but Rafina kept thinking about the limp weight of the old woman ripping away from the wax, the red net on her eyelids, and felt a sudden urge to vomit.

She was quiet on the walk to the bus stop, not even looking up when two conductors got into a fight and began punching each other while their buses rushed away without them. On any other day she would have watched avidly, and dissected the encounter with Rosie while they waited. They would always talk about this and that, clients, the rat faces, Kunwar. Rafina usually had a thousand things to say. But that day the words wouldn't come. Rosie khala put a kindly arm around her shoulder, and Rafina cried.

But as they found seats on the bus – an unexpected gift on a trying day – and they passed the lane that led to the mansion, Rosie khala nudged Rafina and pointed outside: a man in a uniform was holding a small terrier upright by a tightly clutched leash and slapping it repeatedly. 'The dog,' she said.

Rafina felt better immediately afterwards, and began pestering Rosie khala for clues to how the aunt came to be paralyzed.

After two months, Rafina felt like she could mix, spread, yank, massage and flatter like a professional. A hairless tummy, a stubble-free chin, a smooth armpit, and invitingly naked lips – she could give any woman what she wanted. And she had become an expert at wax-making too, achieving the consistency and richness Rosie khala told her was key, by arm-twisting Kunwar into letting her try it on patches of his leg hair before he decided it offended his maleness. He was going to be fourteen soon and, Rafina felt, beginning to take himself a little too seriously.

Rosie khala's facials were harder to master, and Rafina felt her khala was deliberately withholding information from her. When she asked questions about ingredients or techniques, Rosie would only answer so many before snapping, 'Time and money! Those are the ingredients!' or, 'I told you so, that's why!' And a couple of times when a client had wanted her to note their number down in case Rosie fell ill, she had made Rafina tear it up afterwards and told her she was too young and inexperienced to be doing rounds on her own. *I bet she's jealous. I'd be jealous of me too.* But at least she was fair about money.

Ten more rupees here, a bigger share there. At the end of the first month Rafina brought five hundred rupees home and at the end of month two, she'd earned fifteen hundred. It wasn't very much at all, but she had earned it on her own. She had worked hard for it, she told herself. She should have been in college getting bored with other girls her age, waiting for life to happen to her, but here she was making her own life. She wasn't a burden, like Zeenat and Niamat and Kainat and Kunwar. She was a blessing to her Ma, and God would reward her by making her beauty a blessing to the world. Soon.

Her mother cried when Rafina chatted happily to her about all the things they would have once she began earning more regularly. Rafina got carried away and even promised her Ma a new, bigger apartment. On Shahrah-e-Faisal no less. It would have a balcony so they could look at the neon billboards hovering over the city at night, and her mother would never have to work again. She regretted making that offer immediately. After all, one could never have too much money. And it would do her mother good to get out of the house every day even if it was only to work. But she only regretted it for a minute. The next, she was making a list of presents. She started with a modern toilet with a Muslim shower. The squatting-and-lota routine was painful for someone with arthritis, and these days you only saw the old Indian toilets in the servants' quarters of big houses. Kunwar chipped in with twenty things she could buy him in the future. Rafina looked up at her friend on the billboard that night and spoke directly to her for the first time.

'I'm coming,' she said.

But some days the ascension felt harder than it had the day before, or would the day after.

'This used to be the nicest part of town,' Rosie khala mused as they walked from the bus stop at Teen Talwar into Bath Island. 'You know how you can tell?'

'How?' Rafina was up for conversation despite the heat. Maybe it would make her more alert.

'The trees. Look how many there are. Old ones, and new ones too. Only important people walk in the shade.'

'Hmm.'

'I don't expect you to understand who is important and who is not, of course.'

'Who lives here then?'

'Do I go in and out of their houses that I'd know? Those flats up the hill are government flats – it says so on the board. Houses for judges too. The rest must be industrialists or something. It's not someone we're coming and going with, that too I can tell you for free. Oh and that house there? It belongs to a big boorocrat.'

'Sounds important.' Rafina wasn't impressed.

'But why am I telling you? I might as well go talk to that tree over there. Hurry up, child, you're making us late.'

Groaning, Rafina forced her spindly legs to move faster, cursing her aunt, her mother, her diet. By the time they got to the apartment complex on the periphery of the neighbourhood, she was exhausted. Her mother was always telling her to eat more so she had more energy. Maybe she'd buy some fruit when she was done for the day. That was all the girl in the mansion with the dog seemed to eat. She'd slice her fruit with a knife too, just like dog girl.

The frazzled mother who had called for them made them wait for a while, shifting her baby from hip to hip as she bustled around her crowded rooms. For once Rafina didn't mind waiting, because they were seated comfortably on a sofa and served nimbu pani by a friendly maid who greeted Rosie like an old friend. Rafina had scooted around and made herself comfortable on the stained yellow sofa, ignoring Rosie khala's warning look. The trivial matter of where to sit when inside had led to some awkward situations in their first days together as a team. Rafina had not understood why she was supposed to lower herself before some; she was educated and urban, just not rich, she had told her mentor. In some households, Rosie khala had tried to explain to her gently, that made a difference.

'So why do schools for the poor have benches or desks?' Rafina had asked defiantly after one particularly painful pinch when she'd automatically headed for a chair again.

'Not all of them do.'

'It isn't right,' Rafina grumbled. 'I'm not a street sweeper.'

'It doesn't matter whether it's right or wrong, it's just how it is,' Rosie khala had hissed, rising with an agility that belied her weight as the begum entered the room. That was another game, the rules of which Rafina had difficulty understanding. Who merited begum and who merited baji? Who was madam and who was missus? Rafina thought this woman, with her stained yellow couch and indifference towards the asses that landed on it, was probably a baji.

Baji eventually led them both into her bedroom, leaving the baby with the maid outside the door. Rosie turned the AC on so the wax wouldn't melt and be difficult to remove.

'Aur Rosie?' Baji barked. 'What's going on in your life?'

'The usual. Work, work and more work.'

'Still with that salon?'

Rafina lost the thread for a second; she always narrowed in on the verbalising of the word 'salon'. She felt she had to work harder to get the intonation right. It didn't seem natural when she used it in conversation with card girl late at night.

'I don't know why; you know they exploit you. No shame, those people."

'I know, I know,' Rosie khala seemed to be on a more casual footing with this one, Rafina observed. 'Ten years and my salary raised only twice. It's still less than what a driver gets for the same shift, and he doesn't have to do the things I do.'

'I keep saying you should form a union.'

'Me and who else?'

'I was reading the other day that there is a beauticians' union of some sort.'

'I'm not a beautician. The owners must have one. They all know one another.'

'Probably formed to combat the government's effort to tax their services or something.'

'Will that make any difference to our salaries?'

'Probably not,' Baji grinned at Rafina. *She has a sweet smile. Pity nobody has ever told her to clip her nose hair. If my nose hair waved at people like that I'd die of shame. It looks like it wants to shake my hand.* 'I don't think there is any logic to the way your salary is decided.'

'No logic at all.'

'There's no provident fund, no insurance, no medical, no severance pay even. And if that story you told me about the woman being fired for taking two days to miscarry was true, they should be ashamed.'

'Nobody in this country feels shame.' Rosie khala sounded bored.

'Call me when you decide to stand up for yourselves – I'll write an article about it.' The conversation soon switched to a more familiar track. *So my mother-in-law, so my mother, so my sister-in-law, so society, so my husband.* Yawn. Rafina got bored too. *Don't they want to talk about fashion? Not that either of them has any style.* She had to try and get Rosie khala to take her to younger clients, clients without children, clients who weren't boring or senile or paralyzed. Clients like that probably went to the salon though. *I think I just said it right in my head!* She was proud of herself.

'Who's the girl?' Big nose had big eyes too.

'My niece.'

'Her assistant. I'm training for salon.'

Rosie shot her a startled look.

Oh shit.

'You're educated?' Baji asked.

'I've done my metric.'

'Why do you want to do this work?'

'She thinks it's glamorous. She thinks she's going to be a big star.' Rosie khala's answer stung Rafina. Had she been so transparent? Or was she being punished for trying to be sly?

'I want to earn some money to help my family. My father …'

'Don't tell me! Your father's dead, or he's an addict, or he's run away with his second wife, or your brother beats you.'

Rafina said nothing.

'You're all alike, you know,' the woman turned to Rosie next, 'the entire procession of you. Beating your chests, reciting your woes, but you won't do anything about it. Look at this girl. Educated. What does she want to do? Become a waxing woman! Honestly …'

'I'm not just going to be a waxing woman,' Rafina cut in. 'I'm going to be a stylist.' Let Rosie feel guilty; even if she had judged her right, Rafina didn't need to admit it. And she liked that word, 'stylist'; she had picked it up from one of the glossies she had been reading when she could. It had been emblazoned across a familiar face, that of Rosie khala's boss. PAKISTAN'S STAR STYLIST TO THE STARS, the bold print had read. She wasn't sure she had pronounced it right, but the woman didn't laugh at her.

'And what are you going to add to the world by becoming a stylist?'

'I'm going to make it more beautiful.' Let the baji munch on that.

'By making rich people look richer?'

By conquering it. 'It isn't only rich people who can benefit from these things.'

'Really? How many facials do you do a week in your own neighbourhood?'

'Seven!' The number of days in the week was the first thing that came to mind. No one in her building could afford the bottled facials, and they didn't want Rosie's totkas either. Each strand, each family of women had its own version of exfoliants and moisturizers handed down to them. Precisely calculated distillations of turmeric, egg white, yoghurt, lemon, cucumber, oatmeal, orange, rosewater and so much else.

'Sometimes eight,' she added.

'She's very young, baji,' Rosie khala butted in. 'Maybe after a few months of this she'll decide to become a journalist like you. Of course, she won't have the opportunities you did, or the experience – you've done jobs, you know the world out there, what it's like. She's just starting. I don't know about the quality of her brains, but she's a hard worker. And she can learn from people like you, can't you, Rafina?'

Rafina gave the woman her best approximation of an earnest, keen learner, nodding, letting a thin line mar her taut forehead. *Yes, you bitch, I can learn to tell other people what is wrong with them.*

'It's sweet you want to be a star waisay. But you're too dark. Your complexion doesn't sell here. You know what sells? Fair and Lovely! You know, Rosie, just this morning I was reading an article in *Karachi Post* about the peroxide they use in face polish. Did you have any idea …'

A bird added to her rage as they left the leafy apartment compound. Rafina brushed the guano off her shoulder and scowled angrily up at the branches forming an arch over the gate. She told Rosie – who was trying to help her by sucking on the corner of her dupatta and using its dampness to diminish the stain – that she wasn't impressed at all by this silly island. Sure it had trees, but the drivers outside the bungalows were as lewd as the conductors on the buses, and where were the billboards?

3

RAFINA'S OBSESSION WITH the billboard facing her window continued to deepen. Everything about the woman smiling down from it as she peddled package rates was enchanting. Skin the shade of fertile earth. The angular collarbones. The hint of bronze in the black tresses. Rafina sometimes thought she was looking in a mirror. *But my nose is straight and my eyes are better. How are her teeth so white? Or do they just look like that because she's so dark?*

Card girl was the first public validation of Rafina's own allure. She had grown up hearing comments on her darkness and fragile-looking frame from the women of the compound. They told Rafina she was malnourished. How was a body like that going to grow children to term? Raised on a diet of desi ghee, full-fat milk and movies in which plump heroines danced around trees and then bounced easily onto seemingly underfed horses, to them she was a runt. Did she have worms? A wasting sickness? What future could there be for a stick figure? No future at all. *They're just jealous because the men don't look at them like they look at me. Bitter. Bhoosa for brains.*

The few times Rafina had been to the village from where her father hailed, she had been an object of much derision there too. Her grandmother had taken the old taunts a step further and accused Rafina's mother of not feeding her daughter enough on purpose. The son wasn't sending money home, she said, so his wife must be withholding it, and being stingy with her grandchildren too. She wasn't doing enough to fight the effects of the sun on her face either. Rafina had not been to see her Dadi and the rest of her father's family after his death, though they sent for her constantly. She was different from them. She was meant to be a model in the city and not some overworked, pregnant cow in a field somewhere. Not the plump, embarrassed-looking models that dotted the cheap Urdu magazines and newspapers pegged outside the neighbourhood khoka either, (*Of course she's embarrassed! She must know the white foundation stops abruptly at the base of her neck!)* but the skinny, self-assured mannequins that punctuated text in the

English magazines some of the girls used to pass around in school. Those girls had known she was special, that she'd make it; they had often told her so, pinching her upper arms jealously, cooing about how lucky she was to be thin enough to wear anything she wanted.

To that rare praise Rafina had reacted with equanimity, but secretly she coveted card girl's confidence – the way she seemed so comfortable in her body—almost as much as she envied the space she inhabited. Above the city, removed from its garbage, its smog, its poverty, its armies of worker ants. She was going to have that too. She and her mother and her brother. When she was rich and famous and on a billboard herself, they would rise with her. 'That one isn't like the others,' people would say as they'd look admiringly up at her doll-like features. 'She takes care of her own. She has family values.'

They would know this because there would be a four-page interview with her in *She* magazine, and a full page spread in *Mag Weekly*. And the tagline for her when she did a *Visage* cover: RAFINA THE SUPERMODEL WITH THE SUPERFAMILY.

Rafina practised smiling like card girl into a chipped mirror when her mother and brother weren't around.

That God looked favourably on her plans for the future became evident the day Rosie khala brought up the subject of Rafina joining the salon on the bus ride home. After a visit to a client with nothing more exciting to offer in terms of conversation than comparisons between masala pastes and masala powders, they were stuck in traffic in Kharadar. The narrow streets and densely packed buildings of old Karachi amplified the sound and toothless fury of a population anxious to get home. There weren't many billboards here, just little hoardings and cloth banners. Not like the wide, wrinkle-free expanse of metal and paint you could see in more developed parts of the city. The people of Kharadar, Rafina felt, obviously had nothing to express. Billboards were the art of the times.

She had loved that theory ever since a substitute teacher standing in for the science teacher had casually tossed it into the classroom. They summarized the hopes, dreams and aspirations of the people they were made for, the woman had said, and apparently that was what art was all about. That was why it was important to ensure all the women on billboards were modestly dressed so as to instruct society appropriately. No one in the class had seen fit to contradict her. Rafina had hoped she would continue her lecture in science class the next day, but the woman never returned. The science teacher reappeared, and tried again to instruct girls who had known how to hook up gas canisters to stoves since they were six or seven, about the mechanisms of the Bunsen burner. Rafina liked the science teacher; – 'You are too sweet to be forgotten' the woman had inscribed her friendbook the year before, so she didn't join the others in the mourning for the substitute. But something had awakened in her at the precise moment the woman described the power of billboards. Recognition. Validation. Understanding. Billboards weren't frivolity, they were philosophy, and how exciting it had been to meet somebody else who knew that. When she was on one of her own, she would make sure she looked serious as well as gorgeous. Perhaps she could try glasses, perched at the very tip of her nose …

'I've been thinking about what to do with you next,' Rosie khala interrupted Rafina's daydream.

'What do you mean?'

'Why should I lie? When you said you wanted to learn from me, I didn't take you seriously. I see lots of young girls like you. They want to go into the beauty business, but one sniff and they run. You have to work till you drop, and at the end of the day you're not even acknowledged by the armpits you groom, forget about the faces! Pretty soon most girls want out and go back to sitting around waiting for a husband or finding a job that doesn't involve touching other people's bottoms.'

Girls like me? There aren't any girls like me …

'But you're different. You're very hardworking. And you want to go further. Don't deny it, I have eyes,' she sliced Rafina's planned headshake neatly in half. 'What I'm saying is, I don't know why I'm doing this, but if you really want to, I can find out if there is an opening and take you in to meet someone at work.'

'Promise?'

'Slap me if I lie.'

'The boss?'

'The boss won't bother with you till you get to a level where you can actually be useful to her. Someone else. Someone like you and me.' She snorted, 'someone who used to be like you and me anyway.'

'So what happened to her?'

'I don't know how to explain it.'

Rosie khala wouldn't say any more, and told her she would let Rafina know if there was an opening in a day or two.

At the end of the week, Rafina agonized over whether to remind Rosie khala – maybe she had forgotten? Rafina didn't think she had. For all her embarrassing loudness, her halwa hair, Rafina had come to like and respect Rosie khala too. It was hard not to. She worked, she joked, and she never stopped either. Even Naz's tired spirits lifted on the days Rosie would walk Rafina all the way home, and stay to warm the rooms.

Kunwar was a good boy, better than the others who lounged around the neighbourhood, but lately he had been giving his mother and sister trouble. Now that even Rafina was working, he would come back to an empty quarter and cold food, and complain about both. He'd even raised a hand as if to hit Rafina, when she had snapped, 'Make your own hot food then, you good-for-nothing!' She had picked up a wooden ladle and whacked him in the stomach with it. He hadn't spoken to her for a week, and when he did start again it was monosyllabic, and coaxed out of him by Naz's wheedling. Naz had started giving him fifteen rupees with which to while away the time waiting for them, instead of ten, and to Rafina that was a mistake. He spent it quickly on the pool table or the machines at the arcade in the alley by the temple, and then he had nothing to do but squat on the sidewalk with the other louts and bother passers-by.

Ma isn't tough enough, pushy enough. If she'd said, no,

I'll give you five instead of ten if you don't keep your mouth shut and do some work instead of loafing, he'd get back in line no problem. What's going to be left if she's giving him most of her salary to play video games or cards? No wonder there isn't enough to eat. Why doesn't she put that pathetic face and sickly colour to some use? She won't even ask the factory for a raise or a promotion!

There weren't that many opportunities in hosiery, Naz had told Rafina when she'd asked her to look for a better job, one that took her off the floor. *If she was more like Rosie, she'd make opportunities. Just like I'm making mine.*But whatever the difference between the two women, Rafina knew that they were similar in keeping their promises. Rosie khala would keep her word. And she did.

'Wear your yellow outfit tomorrow, will you?' she told Rafina after dropping her home the following Saturday.

'Why?'

'Don't then. I just thought you'd want to look nice when you come to work with me.'

Rafina was buffeted by the crowd at the bus stop, and a man took the opportunity to brush her with his elbow, but she didn't care or turn on him like she ordinarily would have. She squealed with excitement and hugged Rosie khala instead, sweaty armpits and all. She added a kiss for good measure. 'But it's your day off tomorrow!'

'I have to go in for a special client after we do our morning rounds. And don't thank me just yet, silly girl. All I've done is got you an interview; what comes of it is up to you. Don't be shy when you meet her, and remember that no one is any better or worse than anyone else.'

That night, Rafina thought a lot about what Rosie khala had said to her, about no one being better or worse than anyone else. Was she hinting that Rafina had an attitude problem? Did she really make other people feel small? *What have I done to make someone feel that way?* Had Khala meant the woman she was meeting thought she was better than everyone else? Rafina didn't sleep most of the night, just stared out of the window – oblivious to the lights and horns blaring right outside – seeking advice from card girl. *How did you get there, Natasha?* – she had read an interview with her in *Diva* magazine recently and now knew quite a few facts of her life – *You didn't have to worry about this ranking, na?*

As it turned out, neither did Rafina. The woman she met the next day established the pecking order right from the start. She was superior. Rafina was inferior.

Rafina had planned ahead, taking her yellow shalwar kameez with her to don at the end of the rounds. She didn't want to smell like a stale egg yolk for her first job interview. In the servant-quarter bathroom she was shown to by the last client's house maid, she took the outfit out of the bag she had carried it in and hung it carefully from the hook on the back of the door so it wouldn't fall and pick up some of the mould or mud on the floor. She pulled off the kameez she was wearing over her head and hung that on a separate hook. Stepping around the worst of the mess and holding her breath – the bathroom stank, turds curdled, unflushed, in a dry commode – she tried turning the tap on. It made a sucking sound, and then spat brown water at her before running dry. Beginning to breathe through her mouth, she took the water bottle out of her bag, poured a little water out to moisten the wad of tissues she had slipped into her cleavage when the client wasn't looking, then proceeded to do first her face, then her armpits. At the end she sprayed her torso with the Fa Fresh body spray she had bought herself the night before, and changed her clothes; she stood on tiptoe to get out of the old shalwar and into the newish one. Then she opened the door a crack and stuck her hand out for the dupatta she had made Rosie hold while she stood outside to make sure none of the male staff would peep. She didn't drop the wad of tissues in the commode. She kept them clutched in one hand and discarded them in the flowerbed right outside the gate, on the upturned face of a sunflower.

She did her hair on the bus. There was no mirror in the servants' bathroom, so she now made Rosie hold up the compact, turning a deaf ear to the comments from the chichoras behind them.

When the bus dropped them at the mouth of Zamzama and they began to walk down the road into the city's glitziest shopping neighbourhood, she looked so pretty passing motorists honked in appreciation. There were whistles and comments. Rosie and Rafina maintained a studied indifference throughout, though Rafina's mouth twitched when one Romeo yelled: 'Woh dekho! Twins!' It flattened into its customary public line when the next comment, a little more graphic, came hurtling at her.

'Villagers,' Rosie khala muttered angrily, holding her bag tighter to her chest, as if battling the urge to wield it as a weapon. 'Can't get their minds out of the gutter.'

'Villages don't have gutters, do they?'

'Canal then.'

'Wouldn't that be freshwater?'

'Shut up, Rafina, I'm trying to stand up for you.'

'Sorry, Rosie khala, I was just curious.'

'Keep your curiosity to yourself from now on, especially in front of Nawal. Speak when you're spoken to, don't ask silly questions, and act like being in front of her is the best thing that has ever happened to you.'

But it is, Rosie khala, it is! Rafina kept her excitement to herself too, thinking how the diamonds in the window of the jeweller's shop they were passing would sparkle when they were around her neck, and what colour luxury car she would get to shut out the whiff of the sewer, and the love of the witless.

Nawal was an anti-climax. Rafina had expected a mongrel voracious for fresh meat. Instead, she found herself facing a petite, neat, soft-spoken woman. And the salon itself – it was the closest Rafina had come to the trimmings and ostentation she yearned for.

The salon was in a three-storey building set back from the road, in one of Zamzama's many tiny, crowded lanes. It was painted a pale blue from the outside, and a giant bronze R ran down one side of the building.

'Is all of it the salon?' Rafina asked as they stood outside, Rosie khala giving her a minute to get a good look.

'The top floor is a modelling agency and the

basement is a store, but yes, the big boss owns all of it.'

The stairwell was narrow, painted in a matte lilac shade. Ravishing beauty peeked, pouted, or smiled at each landing. For the first time, Rafina wondered whether she was pretty enough. It was an interesting feeling.

'Remember what I told you' were Rosie khala's final words before she opened the small door that led them in. Metal painted the same lilac as the walls, it was practically invisible next to the bronze door that led into the salon's foyer. The staff entrance Rosie led Rafina through opened to a narrow hallway lined with cubicles. Rafina followed Rosie into the first one on the left.

A plump woman in straight white pants and a lilac shirt was sitting behind a sleek metal table, running a finger up and down columns in a register. Shelves lined the wall, cluttered with bottles, magazines, books and boxes. She didn't look up when they came in.

'Salam, Nawal.'

'Hello Rosie,' she said to the register she'd been scrutinizing.

'I've brought that girl with me.'

'Which girl? I see so many girls each day.' Rafina could barely make out what Nawal was saying.

'Remember, I spoke to you about how I needed

some help now that Sally has been moved up since Afshan left?'

'Afshan didn't leave; she was thrown out.' The words had an edge to them.

'Sorry, Nawal, I'm just repeating what I heard.'

Nawal moved a tapered fingernail to the next page, reading left to right. 'Which girl are you talking about?'

'I told you na, that I needed some help and I wanted to bring someone for you to look at. If you like the look of her … it's a lot of work … I'm not complaining that it's a lot of work for me! I'm just saying, I would be able to do even more customers if I had an assistant.'

Nawal finally looked up. Rafina tried a tentative smile and greeted her.

'Salam.'

'What's your name?'

'Rafina.'

'Is that your real name?'

'Yes.'

'Where have you studied?'

'I did my metric from …'

'No, no, I mean where have you got your diploma from?'

'Which diploma?' Rafina was confused.

'Depilex? Mahrose? Bhabi's? Have you done make-up or hair? Massage?'

'I've learned from Rosie khala,' Rafina finally answered. Diploma? Did that flower arrangement certificate they had all done in class eight count?

'So you have no training?'

'I've been working with ...'

'I've been teaching her what I know in my spare time when I finish work here,' Rosie cut in suddenly, and Rafina remembered the older woman wasn't supposed to be doing what she was doing on her own time, that she was poaching clients. 'Everyone does,' she had confided to Rafina in the past, 'but you have to be smart and never talk about it in front of someone who might tell the boss – she says it's like stealing business from her.'

'Why have you been teaching her?'

'She's my khala,' Rafina blurted suddenly.

'She's your mother's sister?'

'No.'

'So she's not really your khala.'

'That's not why I brought her though; I brought her because she's a good, honest worker who won't let you down,' Rosie interjected.

'I see. So you can do what Rosie does?'

'Yes.'

'And waxing?'

Rafina shot a confused glance at Rosie khala, who tilted her head slightly to indicate she should say yes.

'Yes. I can make it too.'

'That doesn't have any value here – we only use imported products, and our clients want the finest, not some kind of khichri.'

'Yes, madam.'

'This isn't a kanjar khana. Call me Miss Nawal.'

Rafina thought everyone probably called her a lot of other things as well, but remained mute.

'She has no training and no experience, Rosie; I don't see what you expect me to do with her.'

'I thought maybe she can help me out for a while; I don't want you to think I can't do it on my own, because I can, but now that Afshan's gone we could use more hands.'

'She looks like one puff and she'll blow away.'

'She really is a hard worker.'

'That's what you think.' Nawal looked intently at Rafina before saying, 'You can come from tomorrow with Rosie for a month and we'll find out. If you don't fit, there's a whole line of girls who'll be more than happy to take your place. One mistake and you're gone. This is the best place there is for styling. I have a whole waiting list of girls willing to do anything that I can't find room for. "We'll do it for free!" Just the experience here, the name … I shouldn't even be letting you in the door but Rosie and I go back.'

'Thank you, Miss Nawal.' Rafina was getting a grip on the situation. She made a note of the way Nawal had said 'styling'. She would practise later. That was the only way to learn, wasn't it?

'Just remember, this isn't some roadside outfit getting on by cutting corners. This is Radiance. We expect the best from everyone on our staff, whether they're the top make-up artists or the boy mopping the stairs. OK Rosie, bring her with you tomorrow. And Rosie?'

'Ji Nawal?'

'This means we're even.'

Rosie nodded silently as she ushered Rafina out.

Nawal resumed her register perusal as they left. Passing the bronze gate to the salon itself – the customers' entrance – Rafina peeped inside and squealed.

'Rosie Khala, is that …'

'Yes, you mad girl, it is. Want to get kicked out already? Keep quiet. Stop staring!'

Rafina held it in till they got in the bus, then the questions bubbled up. Who was the man with the film star, what was she going to be doing, what did Nawal mean could she do what Rosie did, how much was she going to get paid …

'They'll talk to you about that once they decide to keep you. Don't ask either. Nawal is right; a lot of girls would kill for the chance to work at Radiance.'

'It is very impressive, but why? Aren't there other big, popular places as well?'

'Yes, but we were the first to go into production and modelling directly, and advertising agencies prefer to use us rather than anyone else. We're very professional na. All the rest are amateurs. They'll take anyone for commercial modelling. And the money in brides and bridal shoots … you know, a woman from Islamabad flew to Karachi just so she could get her bridal make-up done at Radiance?'

There was pride in her voice as she spoke, and Rafina realized Rosie khala, for all her cribbing about the low pay, the inhuman hours, and the snake of a boss, really liked what she did. Or rather where she did it. Doing the grunt work of home rounds made her ordinary – Karachi was full of other women labouring around the clock to provide for their families. The grunt work at Radiance, however, that placed her above the rest, at least in the salon world. Rafina smiled. She was starting at the top, just like she had planned.

'Radiance did your styling, hai na, Natasha?' she asked card girl that night. 'I can tell.'

4

IT TURNED OUT Rosie khala had lied about her place in the larger scheme of things at Radiance. When Rafina went to work with her the next morning she wasn't prepared for the nonchalance with which Rosie seemed to be treated. The narrow hallway was brimming with other women, all of whom ignored Rosie, and when they stuck their heads into Nawal's cubicle to announce their arrival, she merely grunted in reply. Rafina darted an inquisitive glance at her aunt, but Rosie had her impassive face on. She took Rafina down to the last pale plywood door into the tiny staff changing room

Hooks jutted, at intervals, from a strip of darker wood running around the cubicle with names written on stickers pasted above them. Rosie took a black t-shirt and black pants down from hers, and then handed a similar uniform to Rafina.

'It was Afshan's. She was skinny too; it'll probably fit you.'

Rafina looked at the worn t-shirt, with patches of discoloration under the armpits, and the pants worn from use; bits of the fabric had balled up and hung uselessly from here and there. Taking off her shalwar first to minimize the awkwardness of changing together in a small space, she realized the pants hung a good two inches above her ankles and asked whether she could have a newer uniform.

'So what if the pants are too short? Wear them low na! Who told you to grow so tall? You heard Nawal yesterday, we're trying you out, and you're not even hired. Don't go demanding privileges on the first day; that's the quickest way to get yourself kicked out.'

So today it was 'we' versus 'you', was it? Rafina was hurt, but swallowed her feelings and did what she had to do. When she was dressed, there was no mirror in the cubicle so she had no idea what she looked like. She hoped she didn't look like Rosie. The plumpness of Rosie's body, so easily erased by a shalwar kameez, was magnified by the more form-fitting pants so that she looked like a gol gappa with legs.

They went into a big hall with huge plate-glass windows looking down onto main Zamzama. One wall was lined with mirrors and prep tables, the other with doors to smaller, more private spaces. There was a cushioned bench running along the window. Rafina wanted to go and sit on it and look down, but she noticed that none of the staff was sitting down, but shifting restlessly from one foot to the other, waiting for something. Everyone was clad in black pants and black t-shirts with the Radiance logo, except for one woman wearing a sleeveless, all-white shalwar kurta who was moving around the room, greeting the staff, asking them about the children, the husband, the parents, and the commute home the night before. *Is that the boss?* Rosie shushed her immediately, 'No! Sssh! This way.' A couple of the girls darted speculative looks at Rafina as she followed Rosie to a corner. She looked to the left in the mirror on the wall and had difficulty identifying which one of the forms was hers. There she was, the tallest in the room by a head, except for the man opposite them.

He was chatting animatedly, apparently to the air, but when he turned, Rafina saw he had a tiny earpiece on. Something about the tension in his limbs electrified his outfit, made him stand out. *Is his shirt silk?* Was it a badge of rank? When she looked more carefully at those around her, she realized everybody's clothes seemed to be a better material than hers.

'That's Uzi,' the woman in white muttered into Rafina's ear; she had been staring around the hall so intently she hadn't noticed her making her way across to them. This close, she was younger than she looked, just a few years older than Rafina maybe.

'He's so good-looking!' Rafina said, before she could stop herself.

'He's also gay. How're you, Rosie? How're the girls?'

Rafina had been to an all-girls' school and felt she knew all about lesbians, but she wasn't quite sure what a gay man was. Sure there were hijras, and men walked down the streets holding hands, but the first, all the adults she had heard speak of it agreed, were simply men dressed in women's clothes for money, and the second were just very close friends. Often married, and fathers. One of her mother's cousins, a father of five, spent most of his nights at his best friend's dera but nobody ever called him gay. He just preferred the company of men. *Who wouldn't*? She stifled a giggle as all eyes turned to a corner of the room where the owner of Radiance was climbing down the rungs of a spiral staircase.

Nausheen Ali, a slender form draped in an off-white

tunic, with sleek bob-cut brown hair and shimmering white harem pants, descended gracefully to their level, but merely nodded once as she cut across them to go through another door, pointing a finger at Nawal and Uzi to follow her. Once she was through, everyone relaxed a little, and the girl in white turned back to Rafina, looking up at her with big, dark brown eyes set in a round, pale face under a fall of silky jet-black hair. Rafina had tried to achieve that frizzless sheen herself but never managed. *What does she use? Serum? She isn't bad-looking, though if she was my shade she'd look like a walnut. And she's soft like a dadu. I bet Dadi would think she's perfect.*

'You couldn't tell he's gay?'

'I didn't think about it.' She didn't want to look stupid, on her first day.

'I could tell the first time I saw him. I can always tell.'

It didn't make any difference to her life or her plans – what did she care? But maybe walnut was somebody important, so Rafina asked, 'How can you tell?'

'One, if he's well dressed, if he pays a lot of attention to his clothes, that's an indication, but it's not definite because some men just like clothes these days. If he's well dressed and fit and works in a salon then … one hundred per cent. Guaranteed.'

'What if the owner finds out?'

'Haha! Where did you fall from? In this business it's the biggest asset a man can have! Gays are very committed to these jobs. All the good salons have them now.'

Rafina tried to visualize some of the men she'd seen from her vantage point late at night, leaning into each other in the alleys of card girl's domain, giving some aunty advice about colour – *No, those are homos; this is gay, stop it!* – and had a sudden urge to laugh. She kept her mouth flat and looked at the window.

'I saw Rosie bring you in. What's your name?'

'Rafina.'

'What a unique name!'

'Thank you.' She was gratified. Nobody had ever told her that before. It was unique. She was unique. Walnut was clearly a lovely person. She was almost sorry she was overweight.

'Very filmi. Is it your real name? We had a girl here last year who called herself Durre Shahwar. One day her father came to pick her up and she was late and he started yelling for her in the street. Sakina! Sakina! Aati hai yah ...!' The girl laughed. With her mouth open, lines rippled across the smoothness of her skin. *No, not walnut. If she wasn't so pale she'd look like a dried apricot.* 'My name's PJ. It's not really my name, but it's what you can call me. Nausheen aunty is my mentor. I better go check how she's doing with those two. Nawal is really getting to be a pain in the nose, and Uzi comes with all the gay drama too. Here's another tip for you – you have a kind face and I'll give you a welcome present – be nice to him; he can make or break you here.'

PJ moved away, stopping to chat with someone else before she opened the door the others had gone through – *she didn't knock* – leaving Rafina feeling alone, awkward and more than a little apprehensive till Rosie khala took her elbow and guided her into a room with a large M embossed on the door.

Rosie Khala was a masseuse. A skin rubber, a bone lover, not the make-up artist, hair stylist, wax woman extraordinaire Rafina had thought she was. It should have been obvious from their conversation with Nawal the day before, but it had never occurred to her that Rosie would have hidden the truth. She had seemed braver than that. Rafina wouldn't have cared if Rosie was a malaashi perched on a roundabout at midnight with a portable rack of oils clinking beside her; she had got her into Radiance, the best of the best, and that was all that mattered.

Rosie's workstation was a massage table in the

spa unit. Women came to her fresh from a deep-skin treatment or a soothing soak in a bath with exotic oils in the room next door, or simply straight from a sweaty workout at the gym. The thought of letting other people undress, bathe or contour her body in sensuous oils seemed frightening to Rafina. What if they had cold, rough hands? What if they were thinking of her in *that* way while they were massaging her?

'What a good thing it is, na, that you won't be finding out? Now go rinse these out immediately!' Rosie's tartness cut through the speculations; she handed Rafina the damp towels from the last appointment to take to the laundry room and wheezed as she sat down to catch her breath. Rafina continued to think as she walked across the hall, then made her way down the corridor to the laundry room at the end Rosie had pointed out to her when they came in. *If the water is hot, not too hot but just hot enough to feel good, and they use lavender oil because that is relaxing and I work so hard I should relax*. She felt she could grow to like oiling and massaging, if it were being done to her of course, and not the other way around. She didn't think she could do it to other people.

After a couple of weeks, Rosie, and more importantly, Nawal, made the same observation.

Nawal had popped in a couple of times when

Rosie and Rafina were attending to clients. Rosie would massage them, and Rafina would hand her things. In between clients, she would tidy the room and take the towels to be washed, smiling back at Asha from Hair and Komal from Mani-pedi when she passed them, ignoring Shano because everybody knew that she liked new girls just a little too much. When they were alone, she would listen intently as Rosie explained how the technique worked. A quick study, Rafina had little difficulty with the theory but when the time came for a practical exercise on whoever was free and agreed to be quiet about it, a problem of a different sort manifested itself. Rafina was too weak. Her fingers were delicate, her wrists too, and even if she pushed from her malnourished shoulders she could apply no real pressure.

'It's like being mauled by a butterfly,' Asha whined as she lay supine on the table. 'I don't care how much you say you've taught her, Rosie, the girl couldn't knead atta.'

'Just another couple of days,' Rosie murmured to Nawal. 'She'll improve, you see if she doesn't. Put your back into it, chhota!'

And Rafina put her back into it, and her heart and will too, but it wasn't enough that day and it wasn't enough the week after either. Nawal climbed onto the table herself, and Rafina did all she could but according to the victim, it was like a baby learning the names of body parts by poking them repeatedly.

'Nahin, Rosie, she can stay till the end of the month, but I'm telling you now, it's not going to happen. I'll start interviewing other people; I'm only letting her stay for the next two weeks because I'm a woman of my word and I told you she would have that long. She can say she worked here. It might help her get a job somewhere else, but I'd be surprised if she gets past waxing there either. It's not so bad, doll, don't look so sad, it's honest work. You don't know what some girls end up doing.'

Rafina felt her stomach drop down to her ankles, through the floor beneath, tumble down the stairs and rest by the roadside, where she belonged. She had come so close, and it would all be snatched from her because she wasn't physically strong enough. That was so unfair. She didn't need to be strong. She didn't want to be a masseuse. And she definitely wasn't going to be a waxing woman.

'Miss Nawal, I can learn hair and make-up!' She knew she should have kept quiet the moment the words were out of her mouth.

'Listen, Rafina, I'm only going to say this once because I don't have time to waste. This is a professional outfit. People don't just walk in and learn things. There are schools, institutes where girls learn the trade before joining a salon. A novice might be acceptable to an amateur who has a salon in the front room of her house, or needs an assistant to make wax and clean the toilet, but it isn't acceptable here. We get girls from as far as Lahore and Peshawar – they all have portfolios, they've all done diplomas, and we can't hire most of them because we don't have space. Masseuses are harder to find, and harder to keep, that's why I agreed to try you out as a favour to Rosie, but I'd lose my job if I let you touch a client. Understand?'

'What if I went to an institute and got a diploma for hair and make-up?'

Nawal sighed. 'If you're serious about it, who's stopping you? It'll take you a few years to get to the point where you'll be any use to us, and maybe you won't turn out any good, but who knows? My advice is join a little salon where you can watch the owner do brides or something, flat-iron people's hair, that sort of thing. Quite honestly,' she gave Rosie a sidelong glance, 'the money's about the same and you'll have to do houses there too.'

Rafina thanked Nawal for the advice, her tone neutral. Shrugging, the other woman left the room, leaving Rafina alone with her friend. *My mentor. Some mentor she turned out to be.*

'You can still do rounds with me,' Rosie said. 'Maybe in a year or so you'll have some clients of your own and you can make more money. I'll keep teaching you whatever I learn here.'

'Whatever you learn where, Rosie? In this little hole in the wall? You aren't even allowed in the main salon when clients are around because you look so ugly in that outfit you might scare them away!'

They worked in silence for the hours remaining.

Rafina didn't want to go to work the next day. She had slept badly, on her side, so she could avoid the sight of card girl through the window. She didn't think she could face her. All her bravado, all her confidence, had been deflated.

She went, eventually, because she didn't want card girl looking down on her in the cutting sun and her brother's incessant chattering was unbearable, and neither could she stand the thought of her mother's anxious questions when she came home from her shift to find that Rafina hadn't gone to work. Besides, a little voice had been whispering to her all day. *Maybe you'll be walking from the massage room to the bathroom and a client will be enraptured by your beauty and invite you to her home to meet her son …*

One should always maintain a positive outlook on life, Rafina thought. Card girl probably saw all kinds of horror every day, and smiled through it all.

The tension between Rafina and Rosie lingered for a day or two, then dissipated completely. Rosie wasn't the type to bear grudges. And if she had been interested in revenge she was getting it anyway. Rafina wouldn't not have a job after all. She would actually have preferred Rosie's sulking to Rosie's forgiveness. She deserved it, for having lashed out at her like that. It was just that the thought of having failed her mother and brother ate at her.

It was hard to put a brave face on things, but she did. If an opportunity presented itself in the couple of days she had left, she didn't want it running away from a sour face. Everything she had read had told her that models got work and contracts because of the strength of their smiles – wasn't Noori discovered eating an ice cream in the bazaar? – and Rafina continued to smile. Waves of unhappiness constantly threatened to engulf her, but she stayed buoyant. There wasn't any visible reason to – no client swooped to take her home to their son – so she distracted herself by paying closer attention to the inner workings of the business, and its politics.

Rosie had stopped badgering her to pay attention all the time, or hand her things, and Rafina went in and out of the massage rooms at will. She began spending time chatting with the mani-pedi girls – the most loquacious bunch – and watching the make-up team work whenever the sliding doors between the hall and their kingdom was open. A couple of times she sidled into Uzi's room and gazed hungrily at the massive mounted close-ups of the models he had styled. She took time to study the clothes the clients came in wearing, the colour of their hair and nails, the sort of bags they carried and shoes they sported. She pestered Rosie into taking her to the DHA Sunday Bazaar the mani-pedi girls had told her they got their knock-offs from. She wandered happily down aisle after aisle of fake jeans and second-hand shoes and sequinned dresses and chiffon blouses, carried down the second-hand clothing streams from Central Asia via Afghanistan, touching, wishing, lusting, before buying two pairs of jeans – one skinny and one boot cut – and a plain white chikan fabric blouse like one she had seen PJ wear. She stopped putting kajal in her eyes and started applying liquid liner on her upper lid instead, and didn't resist when Asha took her trusted brown lip pencil out of her hand in the staff changing room, tossed it in the trash, and told her to try a hot pink instead. Someone in Hair used her as a test subject for bangs and highlights. She even let Shano shape her brows. Every day, as the time for her to leave Radiance drew closer, the mirror told her that she was beginning to look more and more like someone who paid to be there rather than someone who was paid to be there. *From the neck up anyway. From the neck down I'm still the girl with the dirty towels.* Thoughts like these would stop her from moving beyond the simple exchange of gossip and information and into the deeper exchanges that might have led to friendship. She was pleasant to everybody, and much of the staff seemed to like her, but she didn't work at making any new friends, resisting offers of a ride home, a trip to Seaview, a treat to share from the new donut shop across the road. What was the point? At the end of the month, it would once again just be her, Rosie, and tedious, backbreaking work. And so her second to last day at Radiance had arrived.

Nawal burst in that morning demanding Rosie remove the knot in her neck.

'I can't take this anymore, Rosie,' she moaned as thumbs dug into her skin. 'This awful politics – don't these people have anything better to do?'

Rosie clucked sympathetically; Rafina listened. She noticed she had grown better at listening quietly.

'This is all that Afshan's fault you know, leaving like that, after all the boss has done for her. But what can you expect from someone of her background? A little bit of praise and it goes to their heads. Thinks she can run her own business, does she? Steal our clients? The boss has been in such a bad mood since she left, and now, to make things worse, this morning Uzi announces to me that he's thinking of leaving too!'

'No!' Rosie sounded shocked. 'Not Uzi?'

Nawal nodded.

'But he's the best stylist we've got now that Afshan's gone!'

'Exactly. And he's saying if she can do it, why can't he.'

'Where will he get the money to start his own salon though?'

'That's what I asked him. He said he had clients who were interested in backing him. I asked him how he could even think about setting up something in the same city after all the boss had done for him and you know what he said?'

'What?'

'He said it was true she gave him a job when no

one else would but how long was she going to milk that? And it wasn't like she'd done him a favour. He said she'd built an empire on our backs and expected us to lick her shoes for the crumbs she tossed us; she paid all of us poorly, kept most of the money we made for herself, took all the credit for our work – what loyalty did we owe for that?'

'Has he lost his mind?'

'I think so.'

'Does boss know?'

'I managed to calm him down and make him think about it for a while; he said he was going to decide at the end of the week.'

'You know what the real problem is, don't you?' Rosie said.

'What?'

'Afshan. They were best friends. I think he's probably angry with what boss did to her after she left.'

'What did she do?' Rafina couldn't restrain her curiosity any longer. Both women looked at her, and then Nawal shrugged.

'Well, you've heard this much, so might as well hear the rest – you'll be leaving soon anyway, but no repeating it, OK?'

Rafina nodded assent.

'She wouldn't pay Afshan the overtime she had accumulated, and Afshan made a fuss about it and stormed out. So, boss banned her entry into the building if she came to pick up some of the things she had left here, and when she did she wasn't allowed in. She had to stand outside. With the guard.'

'But she deserved it!' Rosie added quickly, catching a glimpse of Rafina's face. 'You can't just up and leave the person who made you what you are.'

'No, you can't,' Nawal concurred. 'You have to be loyal.'

They ran Afshan down some more and discussed whether Uzi was just having withdrawal symptoms or angling for more money, but Rafina's mind was elsewhere. It was pondering on the subject of loyalty, and owing the person who made you who you were, and how that worked when the only person you owed was yourself.

Rafina was helping Rosie tidy the room at the end of the day – half-heartedly, because she knew she wouldn't be there much longer – when the door opened and Nausheen swept in, with PJ and Nawal behind her, and started running her fingers along the shelves, opening and closing drawers, and aligning towel sets less than perfectly stacked. The room's occupants also seemed to be furniture to her – *what if she sticks a finger up my nose?* – but Rafina had never been this close to N'CHANTING NAUSHEEN – STYLIST TO THE STARS before and instead of being offended, surreptitiously studied her. Nausheen was of average height, several inches shorter than Rafina, and had a creamy complexion that belied her age – the magazine profile hadn't given a number, but hinted that she was significantly older than she looked, which was about forty. Her eyes were deep-set, bright and furious under thick, sculpted brows, and she was wearing navy blue harem pants and a green top with puffed sleeves that opened like a peacock's tail when she spread her arms for dramatic effect, like she was doing now.

'I don't care how good he thinks he is; if he thinks I'm going to cave in to pressure and give in to his idiotic demands he's a bigger fool than Afshan was. Attitude is contagious. Look at the nakhras from that Salma today. I'm not going to take her nonsense either. You!' She waved a moisturized, impeccably manicured hand at Rafina. 'Can you make tea?'

'Of course.'

'I don't mean doodh patti, I mean proper tea, with milk and sugar on the side.'

Rafina nodded. How hard could it be?

'And can you serve the tea without dropping things?'

'Yes.'

'Nawal, take her to the kitchen and get her started. Four cups for me and the people upstairs – use the special china.'

Nawal muttered 'Yes, Nausheen apa' meekly and beckoned to Rafina to follow her.

'And Nawal,' Nausheen called after them. 'Tell Salma we appreciate that she wouldn't stay late and help make the tea. Of course her family life is important. It's so important that she doesn't need to stay late ever again. She can leave now and never come back.'

'Yes, Nausheen apa.'

Picked off the shelf, like a cutlery set! Rafina mulled over her first real encounter with the woman behind Radiance as she was shown into the kitchen and absorbed what was stored where. Part of her actually felt relieved she would never have to deal with her apparent heartlessness herself. Her relief was short-lived, however, because two minutes later, just as Rafina was struggling to light the electric stove, Nausheen reappeared and pointed a purple fingernail at her.

'Nawal, who is this girl?'

'She was trying out for Rosie's assistant.'

'How was her trial?'

'Not good.'

'If she makes the tea as instructed and doesn't drop anything, hire her as part of my personal staff. She can start tomorrow. She's not bad-looking – always good to have presentable staff. Which reminds me, tell Uzi to give that man who sweeps the stairs another haircut. I passed him on the way in this morning and he looked like a bhangi again.'

Rafina noticed that no one bothered asking how she felt about the sudden change in her career trajectory. But she didn't mind; she was elated. Tea girl was better than nothing. A little more time at Radiance might help set the right wheels in motion. And if she inadvertently became the next target of the spite Nausheen was displaying, well, she would handle that if and when it happened.

5

NAUSHEEN'S PERSONAL STAFF consisted of three people. A personal assistant who acted as her liaison with the staff at Radiance and its two other branches, a personnel manager, and a service assistant who prepared tea, coffee, snacks, and arranged for cold drinks. Nawal was her personal assistant, Rafina became her service assistant, and the personnel manager was Parizae Jehangir, or PJ, who happened to be the daughter of one of Nausheen's closest friends. Was that why she was a 'manager' and Nawal, who actually did all the work, a 'secretary'? Rosie did what she had taken to doing with increasing frequency, which was tell Rafina to shut up and go bother somebody else so she, Rosie, could catch her breath in peace.

And there were many other people Rafina could go and bother now. Her elevated status as a member of Nausheen's staff enabled her to navigate easily between the worlds within worlds of the sprawling, high-end mini-empire Nausheen Ali ruled. Rafina was seen most frequently in the bright, frenetic world of Make-up, which had its own equipment, spoke its own language, and always welcomed cheekbones as sculpted as hers. She never deigned to stop long in the underworld which handled wax and other painful procedures banished to dark corners, so there would be no reminders that beauty cost pain; unless she needed to appropriate an applicator or two of French wax and some strips for her own use. And she was always careful to never linger too long in the hair world over which Uzi reigned. He made her uncomfortable, and she had found his poise irritating since the revelations about his plans to scarper. She felt more loyal to Nausheen now that she was part of her retinue. Uzi's power was fake, put on. Nausheen's was real. Her office had a genuine rarefied atmosphere; the flowers were always fresh and the scented candles were lit even when there were no clients in sight.

But Rafina's loyalty extended only to backing Nausheen over Uzi in any claim to the Stylist throne. Try as she might, she could not match the obsequiousness of everyone else around her, who seemed to worship Nausheen when she was in their vicinity; even those who had reason to dislike her, and were vocal about their disapprovals in private, acted like her presence graced them. Clients took her nastiness as a personal favour, and the bemused tea girl was still unsure why. In the moments she had witnessed, laying out or retrieving a tea service, snacks, water, a salad lunch for boss on a perfectly set wooden tray with silver cutlery, she had seen Nausheen do little other than tell them what flaws they had and how she was the only one who could fix them. An aging actress famous in the nineties sobbed gratefully as she was told her grooming was 'bhayanak', her skin like leather, and she'd have to give herself entirely over to Radiance for any chance of recovering the allure she'd once had. And that too only if she cooperated fully because beauty was serious business and Nausheen had no time to waste on non-serious people who let themselves go to the extent the actress had.

A socialite who had cut her hair off after leaving her husband was told she was a fool; she should have stayed and got herself some cosmetic surgery and not let him touch her at all – that would teach him much better than leaving him alone to pursue his old flame ever would; had the socialite cut off her brain as well as her hair? Thank God Radiance had the right extensions. She hadn't signed anything, had she?

Wasn't she glad she had Nausheen to give her the right advice?

An aspiring model brought in by Danish, the effeminate, middle-aged man who ran the modelling agency and had a fondness for ugly shirts, was rejected outright after a brief interview. Danish, who with his receding chin, small upturned nose and beady eyes behind small glasses had more than a little bit of rodent about him, was practically salivating when he brought her to Nausheen, but: 'Listen to her,' Nausheen told her perpetually sweating 'Director of Modelling, Radiance Modelling Consultancy, by appointment only' – Rafina had peeked at the card the model had dropped into the trash can as she left – 'once she opens her mouth the only thing she could sell is fertilizer! And don't you dare bring me someone with this hip measurement again. We want modelling hips, not childbearing hips. Kasam se, Danish, I think you do this only to upset me. Get out, out, go spend two years on a treadmill!'

In the early days of watching Nausheen in action, Rafina was often paralyzed into inaction by the effect of boss's rudeness on the people she insulted. The teenager had done her fair share of petulant truth-telling, Rosie was witness to that, but nobody had thanked her for it. Especially when it was clearly untrue. Some of the people agreeing so fervently with Nausheen's pitiless assessment of them were beautiful; why were they so insecure? Rosie told Rafina she had never really been around people she thought were prettier than her, and very beautiful people passed through this salon, raising the bar each time, till no one could be satisfied with what they had.

Nausheen reigned over it all, but Uzi managed to straddle several worlds at once as well. He was primarily a hair stylist, but he was also good at make-up, often doing both for clients. He was a man, but he enjoyed the company of any and all women, as far as Rafina could tell. Apart from the fact that he had something they wanted, which was the power to do wonderful things to their hair, wealthy female clients also adored him because he gave them good advice and treated them like they were the centre of his universe. Where Nausheen criticized, he flattered.

'You know he has an English tutor, don't you?' Rosie whispered to Rafina as she stood in the doorway of her kitchen kingdom watching him chatter animatedly to a bejewelled, chain-smoking aunty.

'Really?'

'He's a smart boy, Uzi; he says if he's ever going to be the top in the business he needs to do the ultimate makeover: khotay ko ghora banana.'

Rafina started going through all the copy in two English magazines a day instead of one, reading aloud to herself with the kitchen door closed whenever she could. She also continued studying all the billboards and banners she passed, the English ones anyway, and fighting with Kunwar for monopolizing his radio to listen to the late-night English radio shows. Uzi was right. She didn't know what sort of English she had been taught in school, but she knew it was very different from the fluid, musical cadence of the gilded people who fluttered in and out of the salon, or the way PJ spoke to her friends on the phone while Nawal tallied the day's takings for her. She knew her talent for mimicry would help her in the long run. It had already helped Uzi.

He was the only one self-assured enough around Nausheen to pop in and out of her office without going through Nawal first. And after she felt more confident reading Nausheen, Rafina speculated that she treated Uzi slightly differently from the way she treated all others except for PJ. She was just as cold, but she never directly criticized him. Of course she didn't, Rosie replied, she didn't feel the need to; since he was a man, Nausheen could technically not be threatened by him. Rosie then made a long, impassioned speech about how Nausheen didn't have to feel threatened by anyone because she was just the best there ever was, before asking Rafina acerbically why she never seemed to have any work to do. Rafina looked around and saw PJ smiling at them. It wasn't a pleasant smile.

PJ's unique relationship with Nausheen featured an informality that was denied to the other staff. Rafina, while serving them lunch one day, heard her call Nausheen 'my favourite aunty, except you're not really an aunty, of course' and realized they were close the way she and Rosie khala were. Nausheen was her mentor as Rosie was Rafina's. *As Rosie used to be anyway. I didn't go see her yesterday. Or today. But nothing ever happens in her cave.*

Rafina learnt from phone conversations she overheard that Parizae – Nausheen always called her by her full name, constantly telling her how pretty it was, how pretty she was – was 'padding the resume' and 'doing research' before she left for England to study the beauty business. There were many aspects to it, she would say each time: it was a sophisticated and complex industry, but she would specialize in image marketing.

Clearing up cappuccino mugs from the hair unit one day, Rafina caught Uzi telling Asha he had heard from a Memon matriarch who had patronized Nausheen since she first started in a garage in her aunt's house that she was grooming PJ to take over Radiance after Nausheen retired. But PJ was useless, Asha pointed out. She didn't do anything. She didn't know anything. Well, Uzi told her, Nausheen didn't know that. And PJ wanted to put make-up under her to start with, so Asha should get ready for a new boss soon.

At the next unit head staff meeting, bringing in a sandwich for Nausheen to dissect with a knife and fork as the others spoke, Rafina watched Asha side with Uzi over a change PJ had proposed in the requisition form for lotions. The new form, PJ explained, would simply require the staff to record each dispensation so consumption patterns could be tracked and analyzed. Practical for foreign salons maybe, Asha said, but half her girls couldn't read. When PJ was in America or Germany or wherever she was going, she could try it there and come back and tell them all about it.

Rafina didn't know whether Uzi had been telling Asha the truth about PJ wanting oversight of her unit or just eroding a potential adversary's influence. Uzi was a closed book to her, and she had no way of assessing PJ's ambition or character either; the personnel manager had displayed no further interest in Rafina after that first encounter in the hall. She had grinned at her a couple of times while Rafina had been working with Rosie, but ever since Rafina had become the tea girl, the grins had been replaced by nods. Whatever game the two were playing, it was too complex for her to follow, and she rapidly lost interest in Uzi's machinations and zeroed in on PJ again.

I won't just make it here, I'll make it internationally also. I'll be in Bollywood, and in Hollywood too. In English movies. PJ will watch them in her college in London or America or wherever she's going and then she'll want to kiss my shoes. But is she really as mean as Uzi says she is? Rafina tried to get Rosie's opinion: 'What difference does it make to your life that you're asking? Keep your nose out of politics; they'll eat you raw! And always assume the worst about someone, stupid, then you won't be disappointed.' But Rafina didn't think PJ was ambitious and business-minded. It seemed to her PJ just wanted to be popular, so she was only truly interested in those who were.

Rafina revised her opinion of PJ's harmlessness the first time she witnessed preparations for a fashion show.

'Rosie, Rafina,' Nawal popped her head out of her cubicle as they were leaving one Friday, 'you'll both be staying late tomorrow. Make-up for the Faran Dhaoud Khan show starts at 3.'

'Tomorrow?' It was going to be her Saturday off – everyone got one a month – and Rafina had promised to take her mother and brother shopping. She had yet to collect her first salary – the massage trial had been unpaid – but because she knew she was going to soon, she didn't worry about spending the money she saved from her rounds with Rosie. And Rosie had told her, quietly, to insist on asking for her accumulated overtime too – 'Ask from the beginning, then they won't say you're getting above yourself later.' It would add another five hundred to the low salary, Rs 2,000 for 11 to 7, six days a week. Being a tea girl wasn't the world's best job, but as her mother kept telling her, even after she'd confessed she wasn't even a make-up artist but just the girl who made and served tea, 'At least you have a job, work with mostly women and don't have to worry about getting your hand caught in a machine. Or by a foreman.'

'Is tomorrow a problem for you? Someone coming to make you a film offer? *Visage* wants you on its cover?' Nawal asked sweetly as Rafina considered the possibilties.

'We'll be here,' Rosie promised, and bulldozed Rafina's objections all the way home. Rafina was ignorant, Rafina was stupid, Rafina didn't know the first thing about work, Rafina needed to keep quiet and do as she was told … it went on and on. When she finally got home, Rafina told card girl she didn't mind the sight of Rosie khala's huge bottom in tight pants – *Like tape balls!* – because it meant she wasn't looking at her constantly yapping mouth.

It wasn't as if she had never seen a model in the flesh before. Rafina had seen plenty of them during her time at Radiance. Models, actors, actresses desperate to go backwards instead of forwards. She understood why. Women had short shelf lives. They became invisible as they aged. She had seen that in her own mother. She remembered how lithe and gorgeous Naz had been, the looks she would get as she walked her little daughter to school; now she was grey and chronically fatigued. Rafina's window of opportunity was short, and seeing all those models together in one room suddenly made reaching her goal seem impossibly hard. How could she compete with these women? She was as tall as most, in some cases, taller. Prettier even, she knew that too, but they carried themselves with a confidence she had shed shortly after her demotion to tea girl.

'Rafina,' Nawal had told her bluntly one morning, beckoning her into her cubicle as she passed, 'you take yourself too seriously.'

'What do you mean?'

'It's obvious from the way you moon around the make-up people, begging them to try stuff on you – you think you're Iraj.'

'No, I don't.' She didn't really, she was just curious about how the brush, the colours of an artist's palette would change her. Would she be recognizable? Invisible? Better? More worthy? *And I'm prettier than Iraj. Her face is so broad you could iron your kameez on it.*

'And you've been bothering Uzi too while he works.'

'I just want to learn. How does that hurt anyone?'

'It'll hurt you. It's taken Uzi years to get to where he is – he'd tell you that himself if he had the time. Which he doesn't. The last thing he needs, or a client wants, is some nobody nothing girl offering advice instead of green tea.'

'I only said I didn't think bangs would suit her.'

'I don't care what you said. You shouldn't have said anything at all. When your opinion begins to matter, someone will tell you.'

Between Nawal's blunt warning, and the vicarious diminishing she experienced hearing the things

Nausheen said to those who flocked to her for advice, Rafina's confidence had bottomed out by the time she actually witnessed preparations for a show for the first time. Tall, attractive, pale girl after tall, attractive, pale girl flounced in and she found herself darker and uglier each time. She had to keep running to and fro bringing them coffee and emptying their ashtrays, in between doing her best to stay out of sight and trying not to look down every time someone looked at her. She felt scruffy, smelly, and worthless; she wished she had a nicer deodorant.

She was making what seemed like her twentieth trip to the kitchenette for another bottle of mineral water, demanded in a nasal twang by a top model notorious for her temper tantrums should excessive attention not be paid to her, when she was set upon by the designer.

He didn't look that much older than Rafina. He had an ageless regularity of features that would keep him attractive well into middle age – *unless something bad happens to him, like a car accident late at night after he has dropped me home from his show because I'm his top model.* He pounced on her as she sidled by the couch where he was sitting with PJ as Danish stood before them, holding a phone to his ear and frowning, a half-unbuttoned brocade shirt revealing a sweaty chest and four lonely chest hairs bravely striving to meet.

'What about her?' he said to Danish, but Danish had turned away and scuttled across the room cupping his hand around the phone and his mouth, sweat glistening on the bald spot at the back of his egg-like head.

'What about her?' PJ answered instead, not looking pleased.

'I could try them on her. She's about the right size.'

'I really don't think …'

'Oh ho, Nausheen won't mind. You! You!' He beckoned Rafina over. 'One of our models is late and I need to alter some of her outfits.' He handed her some clothes. 'Can you go and put these on, please? Shabaash! Thank you, darling!'

Rafina stared at him, then looked at PJ, who nodded at her, clearly unhappy. She took the clothes hesitantly and stood there holding them. She could feel the stickiness of her armpits. What if she stained the shirt? And how long were the pants? She hadn't had time to wax that week. If she held them out to check they'd think she was too picky. She might miss the opportunity. And what about shoes? Her nail polish was chipped. Thank god she was wearing khussas. *Will khussas even go with these pants? If they're tight, my ass won't stick out without heels – I should put them on first. I need to move. I need to do something. I'll go put these on, and when I come out* .... She'd emerge wearing the clothes and everyone would be bowled over by her elegance, her presence, she'd open the show, she'd be the rani of the fashion world ...

'Are you deaf? Stop catching flies – go and do it!' PJ's sharp tone snapped Rafina out of her daydream. She scurried into the kitchenette, locking the door behind her, and took off her pants and shirt. She realized immediately she had made a mistake; she should have gone and changed in the clients' restroom, where there was a mirror. But it was probably full of models and they would have laughed at her. She looked around, and pulled the lid of the oven a little further away from the wall so it was almost upright. It wasn't glass, and reflected only blurred shapes, but Nausheen's rigidity ensured Rafina kept it spotless; it was better than nothing.

She need not have worried about sticky armpits and flashing stubble. The lime green ajrak-print pants with sequins up the side came down to her heels, and the pink top was a sleeveless tube of sheer fabric with a sequin embellishment covering the bust. Rafina was dumbstruck. She'd never worn anything more revealing than a t-shirt and pants in her life. She told herself to think about card girl. *But she's wearing a shalwar kameez and has a scarf tossed over one shoulder.* She told herself to think about the models in the imported glossies. She was going to go international, wasn't she? *It's only a body. Just a body. Just my body.*

When she had pulled the clothes on, she looked at the figure in the stove top. She could see her black bra screaming through the sheer top. She took it off. The sequins covered her nipples. *How did he know where to stick them?* The pants were a little loose around the hips. *I'm thinner than the model! I have a model's body!* Or was the model unusually curvy? Fat even? There was only one way to find out. She would ask, once he fired the model and Rafina took her place at his ear.

Before Rafina opened the door to step out she thought one last time of the look on everyone's face when she emerged from the kitchenette, transformed from droopy tea girl to Rafina, the unlikely glamour queen of Radiance. Conversation would cease, mouths would drop open. Uzi, Nawal and everyone else would sigh in admiration, the designer would call the model that was late and tell her not to bother showing up, he had found someone better already. *Sorry darling.*

Rafina opened the door and stepped out.

No one seemed to notice. Asha whizzed by with two of her trainees close at her heels, trailing rollers and the scent of hairspray. The always angry woman, in charge of sweeping up a mess as soon as it was made, hobbled past, wincing, a broom and dustpan clutched to her sides as unobtrusively as possible. The edge of a pedicure tub brushed Rafina's hip as a mani-pedi girl carried it past, and she jumped backwards, afraid the fabric would tear. Was she invisible? She stood still for a half-minute or so to give them time to notice, a couple of people's eyes rolled across her and then back to what they were doing. PJ finally caught sight of her and yelled across the room, 'Don't stand there like a flower pot, Rafina, come here.'

As she threaded her way through the crowded room – darlings and jaanis and sweeties and kisses fluttering around her like confetti – Rafina remembered her armpits were hairy and folded her arms across her chest. She had just made her way to Faran Dhaoud Khan when a blue-haired girl in hipsters and a spaghetti-strap tank top came tottering across the room in stilettos and flung herself at him.

'I am so sorry! I got stuck in the most horrible traffic outside Agha's – they're the only ones who carry my cigarettes and I just *had* to get a carton or I'd never make it through the show.' She spoke, Rafina thought, like that woman in the mansion with the paralyzed aunt. She had that girl's careless confidence too, despite having no breasts, and carrying hips that jutted out suddenly from her frame before disappearing again. *How is she a model?*

Faran gave her a look of mock disapproval, then smiled and hugged her.

'Muneeza! Darling! Another ten minutes and I would have killed you, but you're still in time for me to do your alterations while your face is done. Put your first outfit on pronto so I can start. Honestly, I love those hips. Such character! So authentic! So now! Where're the pants?' He began rooting through the clothes piled on the couch.

Rafina kept quiet. *No. No no no.* She thought about retreating across the room. *Nobody saw me enter, maybe nobody will see me exit.* Faran looked in her direction; his face lit up. Rafina noticed PJ watching with an amused look on her face.

'Oh there they are. I totally forgot about you. Look, thanks for the effort, but Muneeza's here now so if you can just take these off and give them back to her that'd be an even bigger help, alright, sweetie? Thank you,' he called out after Rafina as she turned, before smiling again at spaghetti girl. In her haste to get back to the safety of her kitchenette, Rafina bumped into someone and nearly fell over.

'Sorry, sorry,' a rolling bass voice said, 'all these pretty girls – I think I'm half blind by now.' She registered a man in his late twenties standing in front of her, holding her arm. She wrenched it loose, conscious of her exposed armpit hair, and tucked it back into her side, also conscious that physical contact between staff and clients was taboo in the salon after one potential stylist had been caught making out with someone in the changing room. Rafina had heard all about how Nausheen had threatened to have her picked up by the police and charged with zina. She hadn't meant it of course, Nawal had added, but the girl would think twice before repeating that mistake in her next place of employment, if there was any room for her in the top salon tier anyway. Probably not, after Nausheen had briefed the salon owners' union about her behaviour. No owner wanted their salon associated with prostitution. But what if it were love? Rafina had wondered, and what if it were two clients instead of client and staff member? Would they have been threatened with zina then? Rosie had, of course, told her to shut up and go bother someone else. And that a separate unit for male clients had subsequently been created in another building.

'Are you okay?' The man was still holding her arm.

Rafina took in his deep chest, his logo-embossed orange shirt, his insouciantly worn half cargos, his musky cologne. *Burger boy.*

'No problem.' Rafina put her head back down and made to move on.

'Are you sure you're okay? You look a little shaken up. What's your name?' He really did have such a nice voice. And the way he spoke English … Rafina loved the ease with which the words rolled out of his mouth. Such a beautiful language, such a beautiful man, to be casually dressed in an ocean of gorgeous women where other men would seek to impress. Rafina considered smiling at him – she wanted to – but she didn't.

'Her name is not your business.' PJ came up and put her hand on the man's arm. Rafina felt a stab of panic. If PJ thought she was making a move on her boyfriend, she'd be fired in no time. And strangely, without Rafina knowing why, the realization that he was PJ's boyfriend sprinkled salt on her wounds. *I can't have the job, I can't have the clothes, I can't have the man, I can only make the tea.* Anger flashed in her, quick and light. 'Rafina. My name is Rafina.'

'Pretty name,' he said, 'suits you. Are you a friend of PJ's?'

Rafina didn't know how to respond. The corners

of PJ's mouth curled upwards as she said, 'Oh yes, we were in the convent together, weren't we, Rafina?'

'Adil.' He held out his hand, Rafina shook it mutely, felt a tingle on contact with his skin. 'Oh hey man! Good to see you too!' Adil squawked as Faran swooped down on him, lifted him off his feet and swung him round and round.

'Rafina, stop staring at my brother and go change. Honestly, I've never met anyone who stares as much as you do. I sometimes wonder if you're a little slow,' PJ said, her tone genial. Rafina brushed past her and into the kitchenette, slamming the door behind her and resting against it. She wanted to cry. But she couldn't. She felt the drums of the music outside throbbing through the door at the back of her head.

'Hurry up, Rafina,' PJ pounded on the door. 'We need the clothes!'

Muneeza's the dog girl, I'm the dog, and PJ is the security guard slapping me.

After she was done with her giggle fit, Rafina took off her borrowed finery and meekly handed it all back out to PJ. When she emerged some time later, her eyes less red, she was immediately dispatched to whipping grounds and milk for the next round of coffee. She watched the milk make the grains lighter as she whipped them and wondered what she needed to add to her own life to change its appearance so completely.

After all the girls were ready and the entire show swept off to the venue, Rafina and Rosie helped clean up after them. They picked up discarded chocolate wrappers, overflowing ashtrays, empty imported mineral water bottles, a bloodied tissue and, tossed behind the sofa, the lime green pants, a rip running down one side. *Those hips. Really, how is she a model?* Rosie kept asking her what it had been like, her first time so close to the stars she had been gazing up at all this time. *Does she know what happened? Is that why she keeps asking*? 'They're not stars!' Rafina snapped before closing up so the cruel words couldn't escape. *Faran Dhaoud Khan is a third-date designer. They didn't have the big models. Just some nobodies. One of them had an ass as big as yours. They didn't even have card girl.*

Rafina told Kunwar and Naz, when they pestered her for all the details she could give them about the show preparation later, that it was just chaos, shouting, hair dryers, and a lot of filth to clean. She was glad she didn't have to go with them to the Sheraton hotel too, she said, and was happy to be home instead, where it was nice and quiet. But the truth was that with every day she spent at Radiance, the poverty and squalor of her surroundings in the city centre became more visible to her, and every minute she had spent watching the fashion show preparation had made Rafina hungrier for escape. The events of that day in particular had forced her to confront the fact that she wasn't working because she wanted to help her mother or educate her brother. She hadn't thought of them once when she thought she was going to be in a fashion show for the first time. She had thought only of herself, and how spectacular she would look, and how envious the people looking at her might be.

She knew there was little nobility in wanting to be acknowledged beautiful, to be admired, and be the object of jealousy and desire. Her mind skidded away from the thought it made her uncomfortable. *I just want another kind of life – there's nothing wrong with that. Especially if you're living in this compound. I'm doing what I can, and that's nothing to be ashamed of. Natasha didn't get up there because she sat at home waiting for someone to give her something.* There was another river of life running parallel to the one she was in; it ran deeper and faster; her eyes had told her that was the one she should be submerged in; her eyes would also tell others the same.

6

I'M NOT DRESSING up for Adil, I'm dressing up for myself. Just like it says in Cosmopolitan. *Uff it's Cosmo. Coz. Mo.* But whoever she was doing it for, Rafina's run through her Sunday Bazaar wardrobe was proving to be futile. The skinny jeans did make her legs seem longer, and the tight tops brought out her straight shoulders and breasts, but none of the women she passed in the staff hallway on her way to the changing room seemed impressed. Except Shano. Whose appreciation sadly could not be appreciated.

When Adil did come to pick his sister up at the end of that working week, Rafina had run through her entire western wear collection and was back to her favourite yellow shalwar kameez. He walked up as Rafina was walking down behind Rosie at 7:30, ready to go home. Rosie was bustling ahead – she wanted to look at some sandals in a shop window nearby. Rafina took her time, dreading the moment before she would be at the street exit where she would stop every day and wrap a chaddar around herself for the public commute, after the latest arm-slashing scare. She almost ran into Adil as she took the final turn on the staircase.

'Hi!' He smiled.

'Hello,' she smiled back. *I knew I should have washed the jeans yesterday. But then they wouldn't have dried in time.*

'How are you?'

'A hundred and ten per cent! How are you?'

'Rafina!' Rosie called from the bottom of the stairs.

Rafina brushed past him and sped down, looking back quickly over her shoulder to see if there was any indication that he had felt what she did when their shoulders had touched. He was staring after her. She stuck her tongue out at him.

She looked, Adil thought, like a particularly delectable egg yolk.

Thank God he doesn't look like his sister.

'Don't go making eyes at people like that,' Rosie said as soon as they were around the corner, 'especially not at Adil.'

'Why? He's her brother, not her boyfriend.'

'He might as well be for all the difference it will make to your chances of ever getting someone like him.'

'What makes you think I want someone like him, or even anyone at all?'

'Don't pull that on me, chhota; I've been around longer than you.'

'Why is that so hard to believe that a woman might not want to catch a man?'

'It doesn't matter if a woman doesn't want a man; she needs one. That's just the way we are. Look at me, look at your mother even, we might as well never have been married for all we have to do now, but we married – you have to have that respectability. Especially if you're out working.'

'Most of the models we saw the other day weren't married – no one pointed a finger at them.'

'Where is your head, Rafina? You think you're living in one of those magazines? Everyone wants to … wants to be friendly with them, but no one wants to marry them.' Rosie gave Rafina a knowing look. 'You should probably remember that.'

'Why would I remember these stupid things when I have someone who thinks of nothing else to remind me?' Rafina was irritated by Rosie's constant references to her naiveté. *You might have got me this job but you don't own me. I'm not your daughter or your student or even your friend anymore.*

'You used to be a sweet girl, you know,' Rosie muttered sadly, turning away. 'I used to tell my girls they should try and be polite and pleasant like you.' She winced as one of her feet slipped off the sidewalk and the full weight of her ample body landed on it. She put her good foot on the other knee to lever herself back up. Rafina noted the sweat beading on her forehead, heard the tell-tale wheeze that announced Rosie was tired. She reached out and clasped Rosie's hand in both of hers to help her khala up – *Why did I have to go and say that?* – but Rosie pulled away.

'Come on,' the older woman said briskly, heading for the store window. 'I want to look at those shoes. One day my girls will get married; it's never too early to start collecting a jahez.'

'What about those chappals in black and silver? They'll go with everything. And all your daughters have pretty feet. Not wide and ugly like Ma's. Ma has the ugliest feet, have you noticed?' Rafina tried to make up for her rudeness.

'Don't talk rubbish about your mother to me. Naz and I are friends. Maybe when you're older you'll understand what that means. And are you going to put that on or mop the street with it?'

Rafina threw the chaddar around her shoulders and then settled for staring at shop windows. It required less effort. Her mind was busy—taking work, home, Rosie, PJ, modelling, Adil, card girl and shoes, and making a mishmash of all of them. Although Rosie's words had wounded her, Rafina realized it was the sting of truth rather than malice.

Rafina stared raptly out of the bus window on the ride home, trying to lose herself in the world above the streets, the hoardings and signs, the words and pictures that constituted her holy texts, but they only served to deepen her misery. The English billboards were all bigger, higher, better than their Urdu counterparts.

Rafina's salary didn't increase, but her workload did. The week after she ran into Adil on the stairs, PJ told her sweetly that she should stay in the kitchen in between service so she would be reachable on intercom immediately as, in recognition of her model-like style of carrying the tea tray, she would also now be catering to clients coming to the modelling agency upstairs. Rafina was dismayed at the thought of having to cater to the damp, annoying Danish, but didn't even consider complaining. And she was given a new uniform of tight white pants and a sculpted white tunic with a scalloped neckline that she thought made her look quite stunning. It decreased the volume of the inner voice that kept asking her what she was still doing there.

Remember when you said you weren't a runner at a dhaba? Well, what exactly are you doing? What is this if not dirty work? If you're going to spend your life washing dishes and making tea, why don't you just stay home and do it? Maybe Ma will give you twenty rupees per day too, and then you'll make more than you do here.

Back home in the Gomery quarters, Kunwar was agitating for another increase in his daily entertainment allowance, and Rafina was afraid he would get it, and get it out of the money she was giving Naz. It wasn't enough. In the last argument he had even resorted to telling his mother that everybody was talking about his sister, and it was an insult to him. He'd told them she was working as a teacher in a school in Defence, and the story would seem more plausible if he had more money to show for it. Why couldn't Rafina give it to him? What was she saving it for – more vulgar clothes? Did she *have* to dry them on the balcony? *Maybe if I just gave him ten rupees myself ... but then he'll ask for even more. It'll never be enough. What am I doing?*

She was still doing rounds with Rosie but now also starting to actively wonder how she could acquire some clients of her own from Radiance. Not any of Rosie's, of course – that would be wrong. Though a thought did cross her mind once: since Rosie had so many appointments she was often booked weeks in advance – would she even miss a client or two?

On her first time up the stairs with a loaded tray, she nearly dropped the valued client china service; the hierarchy of which cutlery to give to whom had been drilled into her by Nawal after a mistake or two, and she was cursing the person for whom she was being a beast of burden by the time she pushed the door open and entered, ass first. The agency, which took up the whole of the top floor, was furnished in a minimalist fashion, all planes and angles. Danish, who, apart from the perpetual sweatiness, was infamous for his zero-tolerance policy towards the 'commons', who approached his girls on the side and preferred not to even have a receptionist, wasn't at his customary station by the desk. There was a client in the room, on the low grey leather chair by the floor-to-ceiling window, flipping through a portfolio; several more lay on the floor by his side.

Rafina put the tray on the wide glass table in front of the sofa, moved a smaller metal table next to the client, and picked up the portfolios from the floor to put them on the small table before asking him how he liked his coffee.

'Lots of milk. Two sugars,' he said without looking up. He spoke in English, but it was like PJ's language oddity in reverse. The words were all appropriate but the delivery accented and awkward. Rafina darted a quick glance at his shoes.

She had learnt, from eavesdropping on Asha and Uzi's conversations, how to sum up a client in a once-over. Salon staff were experts at reading the quiet markers of status; they battled to establish bonds with clients who might turn out to be benevolent patrons or even generous tippers in the future; for their part, the clients scrambled to have the stylist of the moment cater to them personally, as well as a more reliable hand who would make time for them in the Eid or New Year rush. Not all the clients who crossed the Bronze threshold came back. While 60% of Radiance clientele were repeat customers, the other 40% consisted of people from out of town, ad or film work, and women who were obviously treating themselves to a luxury they couldn't afford regularly. Rafina felt bad for the last type. They were so obviously intimidated by the way Radiance took imperfection and magnified it till you felt like you were being scrutinized by a higher power and found wanting – they would clutch their bags to their chests and shift constantly on their perches. The shoes were a giveaway, as were nails. They told you about taste and habits. This man's shoes though, they were good shoes. Elegant. Buffed. Most importantly, expensive. She wasn't committing the sin of serving the cameraman's third assistant tea on the good china again, thank God.

She now placed his coffee on the table. He was looking right at her.

'Can I get you anything else?' No harm trying her own English language conversation skills on someone who wasn't born speaking it either.

'Are you interested in modelling?'

'I don't know,' she heard herself say. *What!* She had meant to scream 'YES!' Where had that mousy reply come from? She was nervous. She wasn't even supposed to talk to clients. Part of her was exultant that opportunity had finally come knocking, but the other Rafina, the new, recently cowed Rafina that felt like dung and acted like dung to her loved ones and friends, she wouldn't let the old Rafina speak.

'What's going on?' a nasal voice asked casually. She didn't know when Danish had joined them, but she didn't like the way he was looking at her. *What if he thinks I put myself forward? What if he tells Nausheen that?* Danish didn't put one foot in front of the other without seeking approval from Nausheen first. He scouted out new faces, made portfolios, and 'protected his girls' from unsavoury business practices that sought to exploit them. Or so he said. It was all an excellent idea, Nawal had explained to Rafina, because there were more girls interested in modelling every year, and they really needed an umbrella like the one the agency was providing them with.

'I was just asking her if she wanted to model.'

'She isn't a model. I can show you portfolios of her type though.'

'Show, show. But,' the man continued, 'I think I've been through all your portfolios and I can't find anyone who fits our brief as closely as she does.'

'Then you can't have gone through all my portfolios. Here, have you seen Muneeza's?'

'She doesn't look Pakistani, Danish bhai.Nobody wants to drink gori kay haat ki chai. '

'Natasha?'

'Too exposed.'

'Anjum?'

'Too old.'

'Ferzi?'

'The amount of trouble her husband causes on shoots … it isn't worth it.'

'How about if we guarantee he'll behave?'

'We had that guarantee last time too. But he showed up at eight, demanding she come home immediately. What was he going to eat? Commercials?'

'Uff, so common, I'm so sorry … which agency? That's why you should only work with us. We haven't had that complaint since we signed her. We don't allow him anywhere near her shoots.'

'It doesn't matter which agency, Danish bhai.'

'Just rent one room and sign one client and say they're an agency. Bhai, training is also something. Ethics is also something. Ferzi … we've only signed her recently and we better not get any complaint like that again. I'll talk to her about it. Why do they get married if they want to work? Pakistani men are too insecure. Everybody knows that. I'll explain it to the husband as well.'

'They also don't like people telling them how to treat their women, Danish bhai,' the man laughed in response. 'I think you should not say anything unless someone else complains; it's between the girl and her husband.'

'Fine, but I'm telling you, Fahad,' Danish put on his I'm-confiding-in-you-so-I-must-really-like-you face, 'I don't think married women should model. Men in our culture just can't accommodate the idea.'

'We take the money, waisay,' Fahad said, smiling at Rafina, standing by the door.

'Not all of us, Fahad; some of us don't need women,' Moshin smiled at him, taking a step past Rafina and pulling the door open to indicate she should step back out through it.'

'I do, Danish, I do. I'm an insecure man who wants a woman. If there is warm food when I come home that's enough for me, but if she's just pretty enough to warm me up that's enough for me too.' The man winked at Rafina and raised a finger to stop Danish from replying before saying to her, 'Could you get me another bottle of water, please? This one is ice cold and I want room temperature.'

'Of course,' she smiled, and ran down the stairs. When she came back into the room they were still on the subject of models these days.

'It's the media, you know,' Danish was saying, 'most of these girls wouldn't even have considered modelling ten years ago.'

'Most Pakistani women still wouldn't; it's just Karachi and Lahore girls,' Fahad replied.

'City girls, you mean. But some of the girls who come to me, uff, they talk like they are from the pind.'

'That's why it's just Karachi and Lahore – we only have two cities.'

'We have Quetta also, and Peshawar,' Danish said.

'Don't mind, Danish bhai, but have you ever been to Peshawar? Or Quetta?'

'Not for a long time,' said Danish, 'but I've been to Landi Kotal. Same to same, hai na?'

'I'm saying, it's not even about the city. You'll find girls in Peshawar and Quetta even. It's about the tribal men there too. City girls plus tribal men equals zero models. A city girl needs a city man, aur city men market main thoray short ho rahay hain.'

They both laughed.

'Anyway, so Ferzi won't do,' Fahad brought the conversation back on track, 'though she's a nice girl.'

'All my girls are nice.'

'Of course. But we're looking for a very specific kind of nice. Fantea is the fastest growing brand in Pakistan right now, and our idea is to go in the opposite direction from where everyone else is going when it comes to the model. We don't have an inferiority complex. We want you to buy our brand because it's local, not because it's a local imitation of foreign. We want full desi. But not desi sexy. We're looking for "enlightened innocence", not someone like Bipasha. Samjhe, Danish bhai?'

'What a fantastic way to put it, Fahad – I must remember that.'

'By all means, but please credit your source. The innocence bit is mine, the enlightened bit is Pervez Musharraf's.'

Danish chuckled again. He was also, Rafina noticed, beginning to rub the top of one shoe on the underside of the opposite leg and tilting his body towards the clients. *He's gay!* What better way for Nausheen to protect her investment in a modelling agency than by putting a gay man in charge of it? *So smart.*

'The face of the woman I'm looking for is a face that has seen a lot but hasn't been corrupted by what she's seen. That's what I see on this girl's face. Got any that look exactly like her?' He pointed at Rafina, who was standing by his sofa, pouring room-temperature water into a glass.

'You are still here, Rafina,' Danish said in a syrupy tone.

'I'm just going.'

'I'll call you if we need anything else.'

'Actually, can you bring me some fruit juice, please? I could really use some fruit juice. Any flavour, but,' Fahad smiled first at Rafina's face, then at the rest of her, 'cold. Tell you what, Danish bhai, unlimited budget. Let's do a whole search for the new face of enlightened innocence. Let's see all your nice girls together, competing to be the new face of Fantea. Catwalk. Then we'll shortlist some before announcing the winner. We'll get one of the new designers to do clothes in the brand colours; Radiance will do the styling, of course. We'll even televise it! Kya khayal hai?' He was at her eyes again. 'Any flavour is fine, but the juice just has to be cold, OK?'

'Right away.' Rafina headed downstairs and to the fridge, her mind racing. What was going on? Was he flirting with her? Was he playing with her? Out of the pressure cooker of Danish's vindictive staring, she could actually think. Fantea. THE Fantea? That was one of the largest campaigns! Print, TV, game show, the works. Card girl herself had been their very first face, in 1999 – that's how she had made it big, in fact, according to a story Rafina had read in *Woman's Own*. She would give Fahad his fruit juice, leave immediately so Danish didn't get her into trouble later, wait till Fahad left and then catch him in the stairwell and say she was very interested. Or should she go up after he had left and ask Danish to sign her up as a model? Nausheen might be angry for a while, but they would take the fee from both the client and her and she was sure it would be OK. Then she'd be a real model and she'd get other campaigns and – *think about your family* – she'd make lots of money and they would be able to move out of that apartment and her brother could go on to college and her mother could stop working and card girl would be so proud of her. Rafina pushed impatiently at the kitchenette door in her haste to get the juice but it wouldn't budge. Something seemed to be blocking it from the inside.

She shoved with all her might and managed to squeeze inside. The light was off and there was no window, but she was used to the darkness in there and didn't bother turning it on. She opened the fridge to get a chilled bottle of juice. It shed some light on what had been blocking the door. It was Rosie. Rafina had only to take one look at her face, her wide-open, shell-shocked eyes, to know she was dead.

7

RAFINA RAN THROUGH the salon's main hall and bolted up the spiral staircase concealed in the corner, knocking a trolley over in the process. Uzi shot her a furious look but no one asked her what was wrong. She had never been up the staircase before. Nawal hadn't been in her cubicle, she wasn't in the main hall or the make-up unit or the hair unit or the staff bathroom – there was only one other place she could be.

Rafina reached the top, pushed open the door to the boss's lair and emerged into a long, low room painted lilac, with lilac blinds and a lilac carpet. An oversized ruby red vase sat in a niche in the wall. PJ was sitting facing Nausheen across a virgin expanse of dark wood. Nawal was standing to one side like an obedient waiter. All three looked up in surprise when Rafina burst in.

'You can't come barging …' Nawal began, but Rafina cut her off.

'It's Rosie khala,' she had already reverted to the older, tender relationship she'd once had with her mentor, 'she's dead.'

'Don't be silly,' PJ exclaimed. 'I saw her just a few minutes ago.'

'She's dead. She's in the kitchen. I found her. She's dead.'

PJ raised an eyebrow and looked at Nausheen. *Dramaybaazi. She thinks I'm doing dramaybaazi.* Nawal put her hand to her mouth. Rafina stood, unable to move or speak further. Nausheen began tapping her fingernail on the table. It was a delicate-looking finger but the tapping rang through the room like an alarm bell. Both Nawal and Rafina turned their attention to her.

'Nawal,' Nausheen said, 'please go and check the kitchen, and if Rosie is not in there, find her and bring her here.'

When Nawal was gone, Nausheen and PJ resumed their conversation; Rafina stood and waited silently. Her last moment of clarity was how much of that day she seemed to have spent standing and waiting as momentous events unfolded around her. After that, her thoughts ran over, around and through each other, so that she had no idea what she was thinking. A stray phrase here and there from the low murmurs of the two other women in the room entered her ears: 'Cancer, of course – how else would she lose so much weight?' But she felt no urge to speak, and watched herself, a slender figure standing quietly by a door, eyes wider than usual, perhaps, but otherwise the same as every day, taking in every detail about the room, noting a shaft of extraordinarily bright light, and a hair growing out of a mole on the back of PJ's neck that she had never seen before.

When Nawal came back, ashen, and merely nodded before sitting down, abruptly, on the chair next to PJ, Rafina was still silent. Nawal had picked up a tissue somewhere along the way back from the kitchen. A blue tissue, Rafina noted. So it must have come from either the hair or the make-up unit, where the softer pink and blue ones were kept, and not the economy black and white packs of the underworld.

'Parizae,' Nausheen said, 'take Rafina here down to the car and have my driver take her home. She needs to recover from the shock. We'll investigate further. Rafina, if there is something else you know, tell me now. If you lie or try to cover something up …' She eyed Rafina appraisingly, 'You'd better not.'

Why would I lie or invent or cover up a thing like that,

Rafina thought, but her mouth wouldn't open. She kept remembering the shocked look on Rosie's face, like death had surprised her. What a silly thing to think – of course death had surprised her.

'I need to tell her daughters, her family. She's my khala …' she managed.

'Nawal will take care of that, won't you, Nawal? She's an old friend of Rosie's.'

Nawal nodded, her eyes met Rafina's and Rafina saw her grief mirrored in them. She let herself be led down by PJ, who mercifully kept quiet, but not before Nausheen had told Rafina, in a gentle voice, 'And don't say anything to anyone on your way out, we don't want to upset the clients. You take a day or two off – my driver will note down where you live, someone will be in touch with you in a couple of days.'

Rafina made her way out of the salon, following PJ meekly, fixated on the mole on the back of her neck. They went to a luxury car parked below. Rafina let herself be ushered into the back seat. As the car left the curb she saw Adil striding towards them, but PJ waved the driver on. He waved and grinned as they passed by, but Rafina quickly looked down. Up, down, up, down – life had seemed so much simpler in the room next to the pedestrian bridge.

Two days passed. Her mother had wept when Rafina had broken the news to her, holding her head in her hands and rocking side to side in the way she did when she looked at the photo of her dead husband. Then she had put on her chaddar, sent a neighbour's boy to bring Kunwar home from the arcade in the adjacent alley, and left for Rosie khala's house to comfort the girls. Rafina wanted to go with her but eventually refrained. She didn't know what she would say to the girls. She was afraid they would have known by then that she was the one to have found Rosie. They would have questions about how their mother had died, how it had happened, what she had looked like dead. Rafina knew she couldn't answer them. She didn't have the answers. She could only speculate, and the kind of speculation she was doing would be of comfort to no one.

Rosie had died of hard work. Rafina felt it in her gut. Two decades of constant, unforgiving work. A day job that demanded strength and energy with few breaks, rounds every evening, rounds on holidays. The stress of raising three children, getting them educated, getting them married, for all practical purposes, without much help from her dolt of a husband. He was jovial but inept. He had never managed to earn much. Rosie had kept the house going. And she'd never complained. If Rosie were a man, Rafina thought, people would be lauding her achievements, but Rosie was a woman, and no one would talk about how she'd worked till she dropped dead. They'd talk about what a good mother she had been, what a good wife, and what a good friend. Women were always considerate of the delicate egos of their men, even in death. *I'm never going to get married*, Rafina told herself.

While Rafina mourned, the Gomery street police quarter's compound teemed with gossip. Her arrival in a luxury car with driver hadn't gone unnoticed. The corridors buzzed with talk about her, how she was so stand-offish these days, that clearly she thought she was better than them, when she was really just a burnt matchstick that thought it was a candle. What had she been doing to merit a car and a driver? Who had she been doing it to? Rafina listened through the thin wood of the apartment door before retreating inside and playing a desultory game of cards with Kunwar. When the light began to fade, he went into the inner room and closed the door. Rafina heard his bed creaking. She wondered if all these months he too had harboured a card girl fantasy.

Their mother returned late at night. Rafina, lying awake in the darkness, heard Naz crawl into bed. She heard her cry. She turned over and stared out of the window at Natasha, who was 'too exposed' now. She wondered what had happened with Danish and that client, Fahad. Fantea bobbed to the surface of the maelstrom of her thoughts for a brief moment. She wondered whether the offer would still be open when she returned to work. She wondered whether she would still return to work. She wondered how much Rosie's sudden death would derail her carefully laid plans. She wondered all these things and despised herself. Card girl smiled down at her. Rafina lay awake all night, cursing the lights of the beasts that prowled the jungle below, and the way they flashed across her own face.

8

TIME MOVED ON without her. Each day at Radiance sped along with momentum and direction, but now that Rafina was home, each day just sat there, like an unwelcome relative. Two days stretched into three, then four, then five. Rafina's mother continued to go over to Rosie's place every day after work, leaving her daughter to tend to her son. Kunwar now wanted his sister to get him a cell phone for his birthday. He was self-indulgent, vengeful, and demanding, Rafina thought; he gave every indication of being just like their father. *It isn't surprising; we've let him become that, Ma and I both. We've given in to everything he's ever wanted, because we don't want him to turn on us one day. Doesn't matter if he'll grow up and feed off us; that's just the way it is, as Rosie khala says.* Her mind initially resisted the fact of Rosie's death. She missed her khala each day, expecting her to appear at the door, longing for her in a way she didn't for her own mother. Still, on the fifth day, too afraid to call the salon because of what they might say to her – *You don't need to come back. Kaunsi Rafina? Kaisi Rafina?* – she sent a message with her mother for the girls to send her Rosie's diary so she could call the clients.

'They said that won't be necessary.' Her mother came back empty-handed. 'Zeenat will be taking over her rounds.'

Rafina felt hot, then cold, as her blood rose and subsided. They didn't want to send her the diary because they thought she was staking a claim to Rosie's domain. And they were right. The fog in her brain lifted briefly and she saw the treacherous thought she had denied thinking when Rosie died. As she'd fled up the spiral staircase, it had occurred to her: *All her clients are mine now.* She wanted to break something – a glass, a window, but she didn't. *This is what money does to you.*

No. She reconsidered: *this is what a lack of money does to you.* Before, her hopes had been vague, amorphous, but something had happened to her in the days since Rosie died. Apart from the feeling of being outside of time, she felt a coldness, and now and then experienced a kind of detached clarity. She knew now: It wasn't the world she had wanted to rise above on wings of metal; it had been her dirty, impoverished self. And now it was too late. Rosie was gone. Radiance obviously didn't want her back. She had fallen once again into the rut where it had all started.

Just as quickly as it dropped her, her natural buoyancy lifted her again: *No, I won't let this happen. I won't. Didn't Natasha have to go through so many struggles after the death of her parents in the car crash and the whole dadial turning on her for land fraud? Even her fiancé left her, but she didn't give up. She was the Herfect Face of 2003! And look at her now!*

But birds had been at card girl's flawless facade, and there was a thick streak of black on her chin, as if someone had stood on the pedestrian bridge and tried to piss darkness at her. Rafina closed the thin curtain and picked a fight with her brother.

When she was home, Rafina's mother tried to soothe her restlessness. Putting her own grief aside, Naz tried to make conversation, a joke, lay a cooling hand on her daughter's head, but Rafina shrugged it all off. Naz did not have what she thought would comfort her. She had no purpose, no style, nothing but the crude humour she'd shared with the dead woman. Rafina hated her weakness, and her mute acceptance of the injustice of it all, but could not bring herself to say that aloud. *Ma won't understand. She thinks I'm supposed to be stuck in here with her. Nobody is supposed to be stuck in here!*

Kunwar brought in a magazine he'd borrowed from a neighbour, an old issue of *Stardust*. It was something that would have given Rafina hours of pleasant distraction merely months ago, but she threw it across the room. She had already seen the latest issue at Radiance last week.

The summons came on Saturday. Asha called Rosie's landline to tell the girls to tell Naz to tell Rafina that Nausheen wanted to see her and would send somebody for her around noon the next day. Rafina bathed with water from a bucket in the tiny bathroom, the paint flecks from the walls clogging the drain with the splosh of each mug, irritating the soles of her feet on their way down. *I'll start showering in the spa bathroom when Nausheen isn't around. And PJ. When is she ever going to get out of our faces and go to Italy? What if they don't want me back? What if they find out about the wax? But how will they? Nobody saw me, and everybody does it. My bangs have grown so long. Will Uzi cut them for me if I ask him?* She was towel-drying her hair and applying some of the serum she'd whisked off a shelf in the hair unit when her brother knocked on the door to tell her a car with driver was waiting for her.

Rafina's hands trembled as she forced her feet into a pair of second-hand stilettos. She chose to put on a pair of jeans, and a white blouse like the one she had seen PJ wearing, before throwing her chaddar around her shoulders. Her mother, who didn't want Rafina to go back at all, tried to hide her anxiety. Rafina turned at the door to give her a kiss. She felt a minor annoyance at the people craning their necks and hanging out of widows to catch a glimpse of her getting into the car, but her spirits were already lifting at the thought of being allowed back into that other world. *Which door should I use? What if they accuse me of something? Maybe the DSP will help me. Is he still here? Oh God, I'm going to have to pass that pervert at the bank on my own.* Then she remembered she was in a car, and a car could take her right up to any door. *I can take the chaddar off now and put it in my bag. Or should I drape it over one shoulder? Maybe my hair, as if I'm mourning?*

Radiance clientele tended to sleep in on Sundays, so there very few people present. Nausheen, PJ, Nawal, and two others were already inside, the guard told Rafina as he held the entrance door open. Uzi was giving someone a haircut and waved happily as PJ led her up the spiral staircase. *What if they want me to take over from Rosie? I'm definitely stronger. No. I'll say no. I'll recommend Zeenat.* She felt a pang of pride at what a good person she was.

'Hiii you!' Uzi called. 'Where have you been hiding?'

Rafina waved back timidly. He'd never given her the time of day before.

Nausheen was waiting for her upstairs. She wasn't alone. Danish sat across from her.

'So, Rafina,' Nausheen spoke, 'how was your chhutti?'

Chhutti? Rosie had died and she wanted to know how her chhutti had been?

'Good,' Rafina tried to sound normal.

'Good, good thing you're fresh because you have a busy week ahead. Danish will fill you in.'

'About what?'

'Now don't be shy and pretend you don't know. He told me how you hung around the Fantea client last week. You know I don't like my girls putting themselves forward like that. But it seems to have worked, because the client insists he wants you in the Fantea Model Search ramp show next week.'

Rafina could have sworn someone was singing.

'Of course we told him you couldn't do it.'

'I … but … I'm …'

'Be smart about this, Rafina. There's no hurry,' Danish spoke like he would to a child. 'You can wait a little, na? You have no experience, no exposure. You'll look like a fool. And if you act desperate they won't even pay you. They'll take you for a ride. So what we plan to do …'

He told Rafina how the Radiance Modelling Consultancy – *I know it's just you. Do you mean you and your paunch?* – had worked for days on a plan to make her appear more refined than she really was. They were going to finesse her appearance so they could pitch her to clients without embarrassing themselves, and had worked out a wardrobe she could wear to auditions till she could afford her own. She would also have an hour of conversation daily with an English tutor so she could make a better impression – a lot of the girls went through a similar routine and it wasn't anything to be ashamed of. She'd have intensive private walking lessons from Nonie, of course – her first runway show would be later that week. The Fantea Model Search would be the fashion event of the year, and of course she wouldn't really be in the running, but if she worked very, very hard and trusted Radiance Modelling Consultancy completely, maybe the exposure could land her a small job or two. She didn't have the look for TVCs or campaigns but a big textile mill was going to launch reasonable lawn for the market and she might just have a shot at becoming one of their catalogue girls. 'Plus you do have the right body for ramp,' Moshin said grudgingly, 'if Nonie can teach you how to walk instead of doing thumkas all the time.'

The flood of words washed over Rafina and left her drenched in confusion. *What's wrong with me? It's finally happening … but I don't know what to do! Khala, I need my Rosie khala. I need to talk to someone. Shut up, Rafina, and do as you're told.* She felt the familiar urge to giggle, and bit her lip firmly, looking away from Nausheen's skewer eyes.

'Danish,' Nausheen said, after it became apparent that Rafina was right at that moment actively committed only to swallowing her own mouth, 'why don't you take Rafina up to the agency and talk to her some more over there? I have a bride coming in and I need to get ready; I just wanted Rafina to know I was taking a personal interest in this, so she feels a little more at ease.'

'Sure thing.' Danish picked up his file and then gestured to a cup in front of him, 'Rafina, could you bring my coffee up for me? My hands are full.'

If Danish realized Rafina did not carry out his request, he gave no indication of it.

Once they were seated in his studio office, adjacent to each other on the grey sofa by the window, looking down on Zamzama's hustle and bustle, he resumed talking about how they would groom her. She had to get a full-body scrub immediately, and if she used soap on her face again she would really get it from him. How could all these stupid women use soap, and cheap face wash - it was like mopping your face with Dettol. Milk and honey face washes only!

'What about the kitchen?' she asked when he stopped to take a breath.

'Oh, I forgot you're the tea girl! Of course you won't be doing that anymore. Don't worry, once we're finished with you you'll be making far more as a model than you ever did as a peon.'

'How much? And what do I get for the show on the weekend?'

'What a confident little thing! Whatever is left after we deduct everything we will be spending on you between now and then. You're lucky to have a chance at this experience; I know so many girls who would do it even if they weren't going to be paid anything. Think about how much you'll learn for free. And obviously we know you have a family to care for and you have to eat as well, so, if you really need it, we can give you a small advance that we can deduct from your pay cheque once you get your first job, in addition to your commission.'

'*If* I get a first job.' Rafina thought of the beautiful faces lining the staircase, the stick figures at make-up, and the sudden surge of confidence seeped back out of her. *Should I have brought the cup up?*

'Of course you'll get a first job; you'll get lots of jobs. You're gorgeous – the first time I saw you I thought you were one of the most beautiful women I'd ever seen.'

Rafina smiled back. The first time he saw her he hadn't seen her at all.

A minor glitch in the plan emerged when Rafina's mother refused to let her take the bus to Radiance alone. When she'd been with Rosie, Naz hadn't worried. But she used public transport herself and was well aware of the trouble it could be. Rosie's loss seemed to have made her paranoid. Danish suggested her younger brother accompany Rafina on the way in, then come back again to pick her up, but Rafina turned that suggestion down. Her brother had to go to school, she said. *I'll have to save him from fights on the bus instead of the other way around. And if he comes in here … he'll stand with his mouth open and act like a paindu.* Some other option had to be found. She was afraid they'd turn around and tell her she wasn't worth it after all, but to her surprise a transport allowance was added to her expenses and a reliable taxi driver contracted to pick her up and drop her off daily.

'It'll be deducted from your earnings, of course,' Danish told her.

'I wouldn't be comfortable if it wasn't,' she'd shot back. 'You people are doing so much for me already that I feel indebted to you.' She didn't feel embarrassed at all telling the lie. Whether a lie was bad depended on whom you were telling it to.

The taxi arrangement worked out fine for everyone. It was infinitely better than the bus, and the people in her compound received an unexpected gift: rather than having to tax their brains to find fresh insults for the girl who thought she was too good to come out once in a while and chat with them, they took to calling her 'taxi', as well as the usual sexual epithets. *You'll get yours, you sad witch*, she waved at the most vicious keeper of comings and goings as she was driven out of the compound, *in just a few weeks you'll be at my feet begging me to do something for your Qamar beta too.*

The model walk was more difficult than it looked.

'Walk like there's a string hooked into your belly and someone is pulling you forward by tugging on it,' Nonie told her solemnly. Then Danish ruined it all by trying to show her how to do it. He wanted to show her how to do everything. Uzi had mentioned that Danish was living vicariously through the girls he represented, acting out his own fantasies through them. Uzi grew warmer towards Rafina every day, and by the weekend of the Fantea Model Search ramp show he was talking to her like she was his oldest and greatest friend.

'You've always been so sweet, so cooperative. And you have the nicest skin, you know,' he said. 'I noticed that the first time I saw you.'

It was amazing how many people who had ignored her existence till the beginning of the week had suddenly remembered all the qualities and gifts they had noted when they'd first seen her. Rafina thought she understood why. Success by association. The rumour mill at Radiance being what it was, that the Fantea client was interested in her was common knowledge by now. She accepted their offerings graciously, and tried to dismiss the recurring thought that the only person who could lay any realistic claim to giving her an opportunity was dead.

One person whose attitude towards her had not changed significantly was PJ. She wasn't as blatantly obnoxious as she used to be, but she wasn't pretending to be Rafina's best friend either. She mumbled a civil enough hello or goodbye when they met, but there was always tension between them. Their animosity had been disguised rather than dissipated. Rafina hadn't seen Adil since the day Rosie had died. She wanted to, but she certainly wasn't going to ask PJ when he would be coming around next.

She dreamt about him once. In the dream Rafina spoke flawless English in a clipped, casual tone reminiscent of PJ and Natasha, and Adil wore a tuxedo and had his hair slicked back, just like Shaan in the Fuzon video that had been so popular the year before. Rafina was talking about very serious things to a rapt crowd when he walked up and introduced himself to her, and in the dream she admired the flawless perfection of her face, the delicate line of her collarbone, the lustre of her hair, through his eyes. The next day at Radiance, the day of the Fantea Model Search ramp show, her pulse had skipped a little when she'd heard a man's laughter in the salon's hall. But it was just the stair sweeper, hysterical at the new haircut he had just been given.

9

RAFINA HAD THOUGHT her training would last forever, but the Fantea Model Search ramp show started and ended before she could register its passage. The experience was broken into strobe effect – flashes of light, sound and colour; it was still the most exciting thing she had ever done. She felt so nervous before her first step onto the ramp she thought she would vomit, but she conquered it and traipsed out in perfect time, swaying and turning as Nonie had taught her to do, trying to look desirable, unattainable and deeply unhappy all at the same time. Every once in a while she'd forget the last bit and smile at people in the front row. She felt delighted when they smiled back. She'd been unsure about a couple of the outfits, but none of her clothes were as revealing as the tube top she had wriggled into that one day by the stove.

Backstage, all the girls and their helpers seemed high. They were charged from adrenaline, anxiety, excitement – she didn't know what to call it. She hadn't really experienced anything she felt she could compare their contagious light-headedness to. She might have been more susceptible to it herself if her excitement was not tempered now and then by texts sent to her on Danish's phone from her mother, via her brother, through the second-hand Nokia 3510 she had bought him earlier in the week. '*Kya ho raha hai?*' '*Ab kya ho raha hai?*' '*Khatam kab ho ga?*' Her mother's anxiety had peaked earlier in the day. Kunwar was sulking because Rafina would not take him with her to the show, and Zeenat, Niamat and Kainat had told her she didn't need to come every day anymore; they were okay now. *Uff. Why didn't she mother me when I needed a mother? Theek*, she texted back. *9 o'clock no worry please.* And then Danish firmly told her he was not going to be her personal dakia for the evening, and put the phone away.

How will they see me past those hips? Ass like a water tanker.

On her third time out, she realized the man grinning at her from one of the best seats in the front was the Fantea client, Fahad. He winked and gave her the thumbs up, and she winked back. It was totally spontaneous; the section of the crowd near him whistled in appreciation. She felt her hips move even more fluidly. So this was what it felt like to be wanted. Maybe she would talk to him after the show.

After Ferzi escorted the designer to take a bow, the people backstage – the designer, the models, the make-up artists, the dressers – congratulated each other. Rafina looked for Fahad but he was nowhere in sight. The girls began to trickle out with those who had come to get them, after much air kissing. A couple of passers-by mouthed 'Beautiful!' and 'Lovely!' at her; she smiled and nodded. It was 9:15 p.m. Rafina caught Danish's eye from across the room and pointed at the clock on the wall. Time to go home. She made her way across to him.

'Is there a taxi waiting for me outside?'

'No taxis today, doll, someone will drop you. I'll arrange it in a little while.' The throng swallowed him. More random people congratulated Rafina; she thanked them, and then moved away. She was afraid if she said anything else her voice would betray her.

'Rafina,' Adil appeared next to her, 'the woman of the moment. Some of us are going to get some coffee – come along?'

'I need to get home,' she said. 'Danish …'

'Danish will be fine if he knows you're with me.

I'll text him. And I'll drop you home whenever you want.' He grabbed her wrist; she barely had time to grab her bag as he used his broad shoulders to clear a way through the crowd. Rafina's stomach fluttered and her cheeks felt warm. Things were moving so quickly … she hadn't even changed out of her last outfit. The designer would probably kill her. Her mother was probably frantic. *I don't care.* Part of her warned that this was a bad idea. Part of her giggled non-stop.

Five girls piled into Adil's car to drive down the road, make a U-turn and go to a café on the other side of the hotel that had hosted the show. Rafina noticed heads turn when they walked in, she in a fuchsia silk tunic and gold cigarette pants. Most gazes lingered longest on her. The place had wooden floors, deep leather sofas clustered around tables, and floor-to-ceiling windows looking out onto a pool. An old man in a swimming cap and tiny trunks did lengths the entire time they were there. The people at the table seemed to find it very amusing when Rafina ordered tea instead of coffee.

'I guess you're not a coffee drinker,' one of them said to her, loudly, as if she was deaf.

'No,' Rafina replied, smiling.

'Who isn't a coffee drinker?' Adil put his phone down and dived back into the conversation.

'Rafina.'

'That's terrible', he said glibly. 'We shall have to kick her out immediately; she obviously doesn't belong here.'

That sent the table into peals of laughter. Rafina wasn't sure how to respond. She was being mocked, that much was obvious, but should she let them know she knew? Adil had ushered her into the front seat on the way over; it was only natural for the others to feel resentful. It seemed to Rafina that the two of them were breathing a different air from the others. Every inhalation was a full-body experience. It was an unfamiliar feeling for her. She wanted to rub against something and purr.

'Adil, where's PJ? Is she coming or not?' a redhead arched her eyebrow in his direction. *L'Oréal Intense Red Copper? Stupid. Her arms are so hairy she'll have roots in two weeks.*

'My sister has her own life, T; what she does in her own time is none of my business. And why are you missing her? Does she do things for you that I can't?' He leered dramatically, and the girls tittered. The redhead's face began to match the shade of her hair. Glamour *said redheads have a high sex drive.*

'Asshole,' T flung at Adil.

'Yours or mine?' he flung back.

Everyone laughed, including Rafina. It seemed like the right thing to do.

'Just teasing – relax!' he said. 'We're meeting up at the after-party, guys. You're coming too,' he said to Rafina.

I can't go wearing this! What if the designer's there? I have to tell Danish ... oh shit. Ma. Rafina's stomach turned. She had forgotten all about her mother.

'Listen,' she tugged at Adil's sleeve and he bent towards her. She felt a jolt as his shoulder touched hers, 'I need to get home.'

'Sure, we'll just go for a bit, mingle a little, and then I'll drop you home, okay?'

'Ma will be waiting.' It seemed like such a silly excuse. *And nobody says Ma.* The girls sniggered again. *Why don't you talk amongst yourselves instead of listening to us?*

'You're a modern-day Cinderella,' T said to her.

'Yes.' *Cinderella who?*

'Did you like that story when you were a kid?' T asked.

'Yes.' *I can't back down now.*

'What was your favourite bit? Was it the shark or was it when the robot came and kicked the cat in the head?'

'T, if this is what happens to you when have too

much caffeine I'm going to have to cut you off from the good stuff on our next stop,' Adil said.

'Oh no! Anything but that!' T mock-pleaded. 'Don't take my candy away, I love it soooo much!' She rolled her eyes. Everyone laughed some more. Adil and Rafina sat back and watched the rest of the party chatter away. Every few minutes Adil would add a comment to the conversation, a throwaway line that said nothing in particular but was greeted avidly by the rest. Under the table, he pushed his leg more firmly against Rafina's. Their knees thrummed a closed circuit. Rafina had never felt more connected to anyone in her life. *The joke*, she felt as the table laughed again, *is on everyone else*.

The third floor and roof of the Radiance mothership had been transformed for the evening's revelry. Artfully concealed lighting illuminated the way up. Luxury cars were parked haphazardly up and down the street. A woman in five-inch heels yowled as one stiletto landed on a puddle of paan spit. Two police mobiles stood at each end of the street and security guards at the foot of the stairs were checking off names against a guest list.

They didn't ask Adil his name however, and waved everyone with him through.

The modelling agency had been transformed into a lounge. *Where's Danish?* She couldn't find him anywhere. The grey sofa had disappeared as well. A bar stood at one end, ottomans were scattered around the floor, the space in front of the window overlooking the street had been cleared and a few people were dancing, a mist rising around their feet. A steel ladder rested against the wall at one end, leading up through a trapdoor to the roof.

'We'll go up later,' Adil nudged Rafina and pointed. 'Great view.'

'Yes,' she nodded and smiled. *How do you climb a ladder in heels?*

'T! Adil!' PJ bore down on them from across the room. 'Where have you been? I messaged you guys a million times!'

'Why? I was busy.'

'I can see that.' Her eyes narrowed when she caught sight of Rafina. 'What are you doing here?'

'What's wrong with you and your posse? Why do you guys keep giving her a hard time? It's not cool, yaar. Aren't you all friends?'

'Hmmm,' PJ said, her tone agreeable. 'I guess you could say we are.'

'What class were you two together in anyway – I don't remember her from when you were in school, and I checked out all your friends. I would have remembered you, Rafina. I didn't remember T. T was a real dog. Ow!' He pretended to double over as the redhead flailed at his stomach, 'I'm joking, I'm joking, you were really pretty! Just not as pretty as Rafina. Ow!'

'I'm thirsty,' Rafina tried desperately to change the direction of the conversation.

'Gosh, I'm so sorry; I'll get you a drink. Red or white?' Adil asked.

Red or white what? PJ answered for her.

'I'd say red is more her colour.'

Adil disappeared in the direction of the bar, T and the other girls vanished in his wake, still jostling and joking, leaving PJ and Rafina alone. PJ looked her up and down, taking in the clothes, the shoes.

'If you leave now, I won't tell him,' she said.

'You can tell him, in front of me,' Rafina replied. 'I don't have anything to be ashamed of.'

Adil came back with two glasses of red wine. He offered one to PJ, and held one out for Rafina. 'Don't want any?' he asked, as she made no move to take it.

'No, no, Rafina loves the occasional glass, don't you, Rafina?' A sudden warmth radiated from PJ's face.

'No. Adil,' Rafina ignored the glass, 'have you seen Danish anywhere?'

'Danish never comes to these things. Or he's never invited. You need something? Tell me. I'll get it for you. You just have a drink and relax a little.' He held out the glass again. She took it.

'You like music too, don't you, Rafina?' PJ said. 'In a while the aunties and uncles will have left and the music will get better – you should stay.'

'I've been telling her to stay but she says she needs to get home,' Adil said to PJ.

'What's another hour or two, Rafina?' his sister added. 'You live with your mother, don't you? I'm sure she'll will understand. It's your big night after all. First time on the ramp – you have a right to party!'

'To the divine right to party,' Adil raised an invisible glass, PJ raised her red wine, and Rafina raised hers too. She took a sip only after PJ got bored of waiting for her to start drinking and left, but she detested its fermented flavour right away and put the glass down.

'It's stuffy in here.' Adil's eyes glinted in the low light. 'I say we go to the roof.'

They climbed the ladder, Rafina first, carefully placing the tips of her feet on the rungs, Adil right below her. She emerged onto a scene from a movie. Not a standard Urdu movie in which the heroine went to a 'kilub' and Anglo dancers gyrated across tables and waved the tassels hanging from their breasts in men's faces, but a foreign film with a big budget, like the kind she had seen on cable. She recognized two pop stars talking to Fahad from Fantea and was shocked by how grateful she felt to find at least one friendly face. She scanned the rest of the rooftop. Young women with gorgeous bodies attired in skimpy clothes, glamorous aunties with cigarette holders, men that looked like boys and boys that looked like women and were as well maintained, some even wearing make-up. There was a table laid out with artfully presented food that nobody was eating.

Rafina thought of her mother turning grey in a factory. She thought of her brother risking death daily playing cricket on the street because there was no park for him and his friends to go to, before he'd started going to the arcade instead. She thought of Rosie dropping dead from exhaustion. She turned to go back down, but Adil was blocking her way.

'What's the matter?' he said with concern. 'Not feeling well?'

110% well. Superwell. SUPERMODEL RAFINA IS SUPERWELL.

'Rafina!' Fahad was approaching them with a big smile on his face. 'I was hoping to run into you here.'

'Hey, I'm Adil.' Adil stuck out his hand and grinned pleasantly.

'Fahad. Pleased to meet you.'

'Likewise. Friend of Rafina's?'

'I hope to be,' Fahad said, studying them both and noting the glass in Rafina's hand, the distance between them.

'Get in line then,' Adil touched her elbow. 'I think our little Rafina is the flavour of the month, judging from the waves of jealousy I've been picking up from the women.'

'Adil! Babe!' A yell came from across the rooftop and Adil tucked a hand around Rafina's wrist and began to steer her away. *Now where are we going?*

'Excuse us for a second,' he told Fahad. 'You have to meet these friends of mine, Rafina – they're hysterical.' They went over to where two men were lounging in a corner, backs to the railing, surveying the people like this was court and they were the rulers.

'Babe!' the taller one said. He had short, blond, spiky hair with black stubble for contrast, and was wearing white trousers with a quilted sleeveless white jacket. The man with him was shorter, with a protruding jaw and a perpetually open mouth. They both smiled at Rafina. 'Who's the babe?' the taller one asked.

'Rafina, meet Raz and Shaz.'

'Hello, Raz and Shaz,' Rafina stuck out her hand, and Shaz raised it to his lips and kissed it.

'Oh babe,' Raz groaned, 'why did you go and slobber all over her like that?' To Rafina: 'You don't know where that mouth has been.'

'And she doesn't want to know,' Adil cut in. 'Now that your conversational skills have failed you again, do you have something more stimulating for me?'

'We might indeed have something for you,' Shaz said, his eyes still fixed on Rafina, 'but I think you need to show us some identification.'

Adil turned and pulled his pants down a little. Rafina couldn't help taking a little step back, confused.

'How's that?' he said.

The two laughed. Rafina thought of the louts enthralled by marbles in the hallways of the Gomery quarters. They made the same sounds.

'Here, you can have as many as you like provided we don't have to see that again.' Raz slid something into Adil's outstretched hand. 'Something for the lady?'

'Rafina?' Adil asked.

She shook her head, caught sight of Fahad still looking across the roof at her, said, 'I'll be back,' and walked away.

'Don't go too far,' Adil called after her. 'So you guys playing anywhere soon?' he turned back to Raz and Shaz.

'We're booked for the YGF ball.'

'Yeah? Sweet.'

Sweet, Rafina thought as she moved out of earshot. *Sweet. Sweetheart. So sweet.* She threaded past the knots of people suspended over the world, higher even than the billboards that lined the street, as security and police enforced the unwritten laws of who was in and who was out. Fahad gave her a tentative smile as she settled on the ledge next to him.

'Your boyfriend seems like a nice guy,' he said.

Adil isn't my boyfriend. She thought there were a couple of lines she had to cross with him before she could claim that.

'Who are you here with?' she asked.

'My boss. It's a perfect relationship. We never talk to each other in public. He's over there talking to Nausheen. I was doing a little networking, but now I think I'll relax.' He had switched to perfect, chaste Urdu and the 'relax' was jarring. *It's the Urdu that's jarring.* It seemed an anomaly on this rooftop, but she liked it. She liked the familiar sound of it, but then … *they keep saying 'relax'. As if everyone has time to relax.* Her eyes started to fill up.

'What's wrong?'

'Nothing. I feel like everyone is looking at me, that's all.'

'Everyone *is* looking at you. You're easily the most

beautiful woman here. And you've been shortlisted for the Fantea Model Search – did you even know that? I saw you leaving before the announcement.'

I am, Rafina realized, *really very stupid*. She had forgotten it was a competition. She had assumed she wouldn't be in it.

'Who else?'

'Muneeza. Ferzi.'

Muneeza! I'll never get it. Her eyes filled up some more. *He's looking at me.*

'I thought I wanted everyone to look at me, but I don't.'

Fahad stayed quiet. 'Not like this,' she continued.

'A word of advice from someone on the other side: take it as a compliment.'

She smiled.

'In that case, thanks.' She could see PJ had made her way onto the roof and was looking intently at them. 'Tell me more about you. What do you do exactly?'

'I make people want to buy things.'

'That's what I've always wanted to do.'

'So we're meant for each other then.' He wasn't smiling this time, and looked directly into her eyes before she turned away. PJ had moved over to Nausheen, gorgeous in a white dress at the centre of a particularly loud clique and was whispering into her ear. Nausheen looked right at Rafina. It was now or never.

'Fahad, I want to talk to you …'

'Then talk.'

But it was too late.

'Fahad! I'm so glad I've caught you while everything is still making sense,' Nausheen trilled. Fahad stepped towards her and kissed her on both cheeks. 'Congratulations on a wonderful event!' he said.

'Well, it was your brainchild,' she replied. 'A model search – such an inspired idea! I hope you're enjoying yourself?'

'I was just beginning to,' he smiled at Rafina. She realized their eyes were on level with each other. Adil had looked down at her.

'I'm sure. Listen, I was just talking to your boss and there are some people I want you to meet. Come with me? I was just going to send Rafina on an errand anyway.'

'Alone?'

'Oh it's just downstairs, she'll be perfectly safe. I love a man who likes to look after women though – why don't you come and charm some of my friends over there?'

'I need to go home anyway,' Rafina said. The

moment was lost. She'd tried to change the equation and failed. Even if she managed to talk to Fahad in detail, he would probably be reluctant to bypass the agency and Nausheen.

'That's just where I was sending you, Rafina. Go downstairs to the salon and ask Nawal to arrange a ride.'

'Nawal is here?'

'She's downstairs, of course. Now move, come on, and let's see that walk you were doing so well earlier in the evening.'

'I should probably tell the people I came with …'

'I'll take care of it. You came with PJ's brother, didn't you? I heard all about it. You have initiative, I'll give you that.' Nausheen wrapped an arm around Fahad's arm. 'Now let's see what we can do with you.'

Rafina looked for Adil, and saw that he was still standing in the corner laughing with Raz and Shaz. PJ had positioned herself conveniently in between and gave her a friendly little wave while mouthing 'Buhbye.'

Rafina made her way down the ladder and into the stairwell. The party had really taken off now, and spilled onto the staircase. A girl leaned backwards into a man leaning against a wall, others chatted with glasses empty and full, cigarettes clutched in hands.

Laughter seemed to be coming from everywhere and nowhere. The lights shimmering along the bases of the steps threw the faces on the mounted magazine covers on each landing into shadow.

She let herself into the salon through the staff door. Inside, it was deathly quiet. She checked in Nawal's office but it was empty. So was the main hall. She even checked in Nausheen's office but Nawal wasn't there either. She stood in the hall and called out her name but there was no answer. *She must have left.* Rafina was on her own. She'd have to make her way home by herself. How much money did she have? Not enough for a taxi. And it was too late for a bus. There was no way she could take a rickshaw in the clothes she was wearing, plus she'd have to walk a long way to find one.

She decided to borrow someone's work outfit. Black jeans and t-shirt would be better than what she was wearing. Her own clothes were in her tote bag, which was in Adil's car. She couldn't face going back up there and running into Nausheen and PJ again. She made her way down the corridor and opened the door to the changing cubicle. It was pitch dark; she fumbled for the light and turned it on.

Nawal was sitting on the floor in a corner. She was wearing a rumpled shalwar kameez, no dupatta, and she had obviously been crying. There was something clutched tightly in her hands. It was a black t-shirt. She was holding it to her nose, inhaling its scent. She looked up when Rafina turned the light on and squinted at her.

'Nawal?'

'She was my best friend, you know,' Nawal spoke into the air, to the opposite wall. Rafina sank to her knees beside her.

'Who?'

'Rosie. We joined together. We were inseparable when we started. Then I got promoted, and caught up, and turned mean and spiteful and full of myself.'

'Don't say that, Nawal.'

'Why not? It's true. I was so excited the first time Nausheen gave me her cast-offs, her clothes, even her shoes. I thought it was a sign of favour. And it was.'

'She appreciates you.'

'Of course she does. These sort of people appreciate their dogs even. That's what I am – I'm her pet bitch.'

'Let's go home, Nawal.' Rafina thought it would be easier for her if there were two of them looking for transport this late at night.

'You know what I had to do the day Rosie died and they sent you home? I went downstairs, I lit scented candles, locked the kitchen from outside. I locked Rosie in. She lay there till the workday was over so no one would know. Then the driver and the guard wrapped her in a sheet and I got in the car with her and took her home. I told her family she had died in the evening. I gave them one lakh from Nausheen to say it had happened at home – a natural death.

Rafina sank onto the floor next to Nawal and stared at the wall with her. Rosie had lain there all day, alone? If she had known, she would have stayed with her.

'One lakh. That was the price of Rosie's dignity. Mine was free, of course – I lost it a long time ago.'

'Let me take you home, Nawal.' If Nawal did something stupid Rafina felt she would have to take care of her, for Rosie's sake. Rosie had been her friend too. Rafina hadn't behaved any better towards her than Nawal had; she shared her guilt, but sitting in the dark whining about it while hopes of finding a rickshaw got slimmer and slimmer, wasn't helping anyone.

'Don't talk to me like I'm a child, you stupid girl.'

'I'm just trying to help!' Rafina was surprised by the edge to Nawal's voice.

'Who are you to offer me help? Talk to me like that again and I'll have you fired.' Nawal got to her feet and tossed the shirt to the ground. 'You think I can't? I can do anything I like here – anything; I have

Nausheen wrapped around my little finger. You think a girl like you can come in here and give me lip? Get out! Get out of my cubicle!'

Rafina, her arms prickling in gooseflesh, fled. She stumbled down the stairs, numb, ran past the security guards, past the police mobiles at the corner and onto the street. She had walked just a few yards, panic finally rising in her, panic and anger at humiliation after humiliation, when a car pulled to the curb next to her.

It was Fahad. He opened the car door for her and she clambered in.

'Which way?' he asked.

'You know that big Welcom Telcom billboard on M. A. Jinnah?'

He nodded. Of course he would.

'There.'

10

'DANISH?' RAFINA MADE the call from her new cell phone as her brother waited by the roadside with her. 'I need to see you. Yes, yes, I know I've missed two sessions with the tutor – that's part of what I want to talk to you about. When? OK, I'll be there in an hour.'

'Go inside,' she pushed Kunwar. 'Tell Ma I'll be back in the evening.'

She hailed a rickshaw. There was a new confidence about her, an ease to the way her arms swung out from her torso and the way her legs stretched across the gutter grate as she stepped down from the pavement.

Rafina bypassed the bronze gate, the staff entrance and went straight up to the third floor. Danish was alone, but he made her wait for a while anyway. Answering calls, studying portfolios, making little humming sounds. Rafina sat absolutely still and made no demands of him.

'Well, Rafina,' he looked up at her finally, 'how have you been?'

'Fine, thank you, Danish. What about you?'

'Fine. We thought you were sick when you didn't show up on Monday.'

'I wasn't.'

'And nobody was answering the phone we got you. Nausheen was quite angry. She felt, and I agree with her, that it really doesn't show a lot of gratitude for the investment we've made in you.'

'She didn't seem that unhappy when I met her last.'

'When did you meet her last? I saw her just a little while ago.'

'At the after-party on Sunday, of course, but you weren't invited to that, were you, Danish?'

'I was busy.'

'Waiting to be called? It'll never happen, you know.'

Danish sat back, stunned. He took in the young woman across from him. The straight, unbowed shoulders, the direct gaze. 'I think you're going off track,' he said.

'No, I know exactly where I'm going.'

'You'll be going out of that door in a minute.'

'OK.' She got up to leave.

'Where are you going?'

'Out of that door like you told me to.'

'Stop this stupidity and sit down.'

'I don't want to. I think I'm done here.'

'You owe us money. You're not done till we say you're done.'

Rafina opened her new yellow handbag and dumped an envelope on his desk; he could see the crisp notes inside.

'I wonder what you did to get this,' Danish said, his voice nasty.

'Signed a contract to be the new Fantea girl actually.'

He sat with his mouth open for what seemed like a full minute to Rafina. Expressions she couldn't place flitted across his face. *Is he impressed or angry or constipated?* 'You can't do that – that has to be done through us! We're their agency. We're your agency!'

'But Danish, you never had me sign anything. You didn't think I could write my own name. I'll stop and say bye to Nawal too on my way down, and return the clothes I was wearing after the show and pick up a bag I left behind.'

He was picking up his phone as she headed for the stairs. Someone was singing again – she could hear it very clearly.

Rafina pulled the bag containing the fuschia tunic and gold pants closer to her chest and took a deep breath before pressing the buzzer by the bronze gate. The camera above the door swivelled towards her. The security system ensured no undesirable visitors were able to gain entrance to the hallowed halls within, unless, of course, they came through the staff door. The camera remained fixed on her, then turned away. The door remained sealed. Rafina buzzed again. A woman with her daughter came up the stairs and pressed the buzzer, the camera turned towards them and the door swung open. They stepped inside, Rafina caught the door before it shut and was about to step inside when Uzi loomed up before her.

'Use the other door,' he told her, in Urdu. Rafina could see PJ smirking by the reception desk behind him.

'Never mind,' Rafina said as she pressed the bag into his chest. 'Tell them I want that bag of mine with the jora inside.'

She waited outside in the sun for an hour but they wouldn't return her clothes. She told herself it didn't matter but as she decided to leave, her vision blurred with tears and she dropped her purse while crossing the road. The rickshaw-wala she had contracted to wait got down from his rickshaw to help her gather her things, but she didn't want any help.

'Why don't you mind your own business and stick to doing what you're being paid to do!' she exploded in his face.

Over the next month the teasers from the Fantea campaign led to offers for TV and music videos. Rafina was in talks about a shampoo campaign, and there was a possibility she would also be one of the new TW phone card girls. Zeenat asked Naz to convince Rafina to take her on as her personal assistant on shoots, but Rafina didn't think she owed Zeenat anything. Besides, the girl was cheap.

Fahad was functioning as her unofficial booker. She trusted him more each day. He had helped her find the flat overlooking Shahrah-e-Faisal to which she and her family were moving. He wasn't rough when they had sex, and once, after she put on the clothes worn by the last Fantea model and knelt down to suck his cock for a little while, he had told her she was even better than Natasha. It made Rafina happy. She felt uplifted by the comparison, even if Natasha hadn't been as popular since a mob of rampaging madrassa students attacked the card girl billboard and set fire to it.

Acknowledgements

THIS NOVELLA WAS written in 2004, and has surfaced now thanks to the encouragement of Imran Yusuf and Kanishka Gupta, and the editorial vision of Teesta Guha Sarkar.